SECOND DOWN Scrooge

LISA SUZANNE

SECOND DOWN SCROOGE
© LISA SUZANNE 2024

Published in the United States of America by Books by LS, LLC.

ISBN: 978-1-963772-13-5

Books by Lisa Suzanne

THE NASH BROTHERS
Dating the Defensive Back
Wedding the Wide Receiver

VEGAS ACES
Home Game (Book One)
Long Game (Book Two)
Fair Game (Book Three)
Waiting Game (Book Four)
End Game (Book Five)

VEGAS ACES: THE QUARTERBACK
Traded (Book One)
Tackled (Book Two)
Timeout (Book Three)
Turnover (Book Four)
Touchdown (Book Five)

VEGAS ACES: THE TIGHT END
Tight Spot (Book One)
Tight Hold (Book Two)
Tight Fit (Book Three)
Tight Laced (Book Four)
Tight End (Book Five)

Visit Lisa on Amazon for more titles

Dedication

To the three people who fill me with holiday cheer
every day of the year.

Chapter 1
Kelly Kaplan

Darling Christmas Cookie Wreaths

Four Weeks Until Christmas

"Cookie's Cookies and Cakes, this is Kelly speaking." I blow a breath upward in some attempt to push my hair out of my eyes, and I glance over at the baby corner under the windows in my office. Soon enough, we're going to have to turn it into a *toddler* corner. Mia is crawling all over the place at ten months, and soon she'll be walking, and…then I guess I can't confine her to a corner in my office anymore.

"Hey. It's me."

My chest tightens as I hear his voice. It shouldn't tighten. I should be past all this by now, ready to move on with some hot new hunk.

I'm not ready, and I wish I knew why he's calling me at work rather than on my phone.

5

"Why didn't you just call my phone?" I ask. It's throwing me off to be on my office line with him rather than on my phone.

"I did. It went to voicemail."

I glance at my desk as I look for my phone, and I don't even see it. I have Christmas music playing while I work on a set of wreaths to hang up in the shop, and I have little faux cookies and cakes scattered all over my desk. I decorated those with red and green paint yesterday, and I'm hot-gluing them on the wreaths today.

I move some red and green ribbon, and voila…there's the phone.

I pick it up and spot the missed call.

"Sorry," I mutter. "I'm in the middle of something. What do you need?"

"I, uh, sorry, but I can't do next Tuesday with Mia." He sounds apologetic, and it's rare he misses time with Mia, but that doesn't make the feeling of being let down any less brutal. "I got invited to this charity thing, and the entire coaching staff will be there, so I need to make sure to put in my time. Our offensive coordinator is big on face time off the field." He sounds annoyed by that fact.

"Okay," I mutter with a sigh. It's not that I mind being with Mia twenty-four seven. I adore her. She's my entire world. She's my littlest best friend, which is why I nicknamed her Miamiga— like mi amiga. It just came out one day, and it stuck.

It's just that Tuesdays are when I book all my appointments so I don't have to drag the baby along with me, and I scheduled a haircut and my annual exam this Tuesday. It's Austin's one day off each week, and he always spends it with his little girl.

I guess I'm either canceling or Mia's coming with me. Good thing she's young enough not to remember her mom's feet in stirrups with my legs spread eagle as a doctor sticks various items up my hoo-ha.

"I'm sorry. Don't be mad. Can I make it up to you by spending some time with her after practice on Friday?" he asks.

"That's fine." I yank on some of the mesh that looks crooked. "I guess I'll see you then."

"Are you ready to give this another chance yet?" he asks.

I chuckle. He ends pretty much every conversation the same way.

It's not that I don't want to give him a chance. The way my chest tightened when his voice took me off guard tells me I still have feelings for him. Strong ones. Usually I can manage them better when I see his name flash on my phone screen as if it's serving as a warning, and this time I was just caught off guard.

We have a history. He betrayed my best friend and her husband when he secretly recorded a private conversation and sold it to the highest bidder, and I can't get past that. I'm nothing if not a loyal friend. I already had trust issues, ones he was aware of, and he swooped in and proved I couldn't trust him. If he could hurt my friends, how can I be sure I'm not next on his list?

I may be a generally optimistic and positive person, but that doesn't mean I hand out my trust easily.

There's way less risk to my heart by keeping him at arm's length. I've done it for a year and a half now, and I don't see that changing anytime soon.

That's not to say I wouldn't want another night or two with him. We could have some fun and keep our emotions in check...right?

Wrong.

I know it's wrong because we tried it. There's a little voice in the back of my head that reminds me of that fact whenever I get any silly ideas that we could make it work.

We can't. We tried. We failed. That's that.

"Not yet," I say lightly.

"Fine," he mutters. "I'll talk to you soon."

I hang up and finish the wreath, and I spot Mia climbing into her bouncy chair, her tiny ponytail made out of the little whisps of hair I gathered up on top of her head swinging with her movements. That's usually the signal that she's tired and ready for a nap, so I walk over, pick her up, and snuggle her to my chest. "Daddy said he'll see you Friday, baby girl," I murmur.

I walk over to the rocking chair Ava ordered for my office, and I sit down and start to rock her. Her eyes close, and once I'm certain she's asleep, I set her in the bassinet that she's nearly starting to outgrow.

I take my wreath and my baby monitor, and I head out of my office, lock the door, and walk out toward the cafe, where I find Ava talking to some customers over the counter. Once they're done, I show her the wreath.

"God, Kel. You're so talented. I wish I had half the creativity you do."

"You totally do. Your cookies are the cutest in town." I nod toward the case of cookies. The hottest sellers right now are the Vegas Aces cookies she's been making with the team logo since her husband is a former player on the team. In fact, the night she met him—or *re*-met him, I guess, since she'd known him since she was a kid but hadn't seen him in a decade—was the same night I met Austin. It was a year and a half ago now, but she's married, and I'm…not.

I'm an exhausted single mom.

We had a fling, we had some fun, and I ended up pregnant. And that's pretty much the end of our story. He did some underhanded things, I found out he was a member of a sex club, and I can't be anything more than a co-parent with him.

And flaking on our standing Tuesday appointment feels like a step backward instead of forward.

He's in season, though, so I'm trying to be understanding.

"Oh, that wreath is just darling!" Mrs. Howard says from the other side of the counter. "How much is it?"

"Oh, no, these aren't for sale," I say. "Just decorations I made for Ava." I hang it on the wall behind the register where we always hang a wreath for whatever holiday is coming next. It's the

Saturday after Thanksgiving, so all the Christmas décor is going up today.

"I'd pay fifty for one," Mrs. Howard says. "And so would every other lady in my bunco group."

I glance over at her in surprise. "Really?"

She nods. "Really. They're just adorable…and so are you. In fact, you'd be perfect for my grandson. Are you seeing anybody?"

Gotta hand it to grandmas. Somehow, they just know the exact most awkward thing to say.

"Oh, I'm not really dating right now," I decline respectfully. "Single mom, busy work schedule, you know how it goes." I duck my head in embarrassment.

"I do. All the more reason to get you out to have a little fun. How's Friday?" she asks.

"Your cakes are ready," Callie says as she walks in from the kitchen with two boxes, and I'm thankful for the interruption.

"Thank you, honey," Mrs. Howard says. Jenny follows behind Callie with two more boxes, and Mrs. Howard looks at me. "Would you help me get these out to my car, dear?"

I nod. "Of course."

I carry two boxes, and she carries the other two. I carefully set them in the trunk of her Lincoln.

"Now about Friday. Max can pick you up from here or at your house around, say…seven?"

"Mrs. Howard! Don't be silly. You didn't even check with Max to see if he's free."

She laughs. "He's got dinner plans with me on Friday at seven." She leans in toward me. "I'm just swapping out *me* for you."

"I'm sure he'd really appreciate that, but I can't. Really." Except…I can. Austin just called to tell me that he wants to spend time with Mia on Friday after practice, and he didn't say anything about *me* being there. And why not get picked up for a date while he's there? Maybe it'll send him the message I'm trying to send.

Except, to be honest, I'm not even sure what that message is at this point.

I'm holding him at arm's length even though I want him. I'm half in love with him, half in hate with him. I'm still angry that he hurt my friend, his priorities are not aligned with mine, and I'm trying to move on, but I can't since we see each other at a minimum of once a week with this whole co-parenting thing, and I'm still *so* attracted to him that it's unreal.

I can't stay stuck in neutral forever. I should *do* something about it.

"He's a real catch, but I understand," she says. She smiles warmly at me, and then she walks toward the driver's side of her car.

Moving on. The message I want to send is that it's time for me to *move on*.

"Okay," I sort of yelp in agreement before she leaves, surprising even myself at my outburst. She stops and looks up at me. "Okay, I'll go out with him."

Her lips break out into a broad smile. "That's wonderful."

I give her my number and tell her to have Max text me, and then I wonder what the hell I just agreed to.

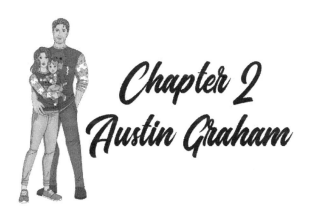

Chapter 2
Austin Graham

Another Christmas I'll Spend Alone

Four Weeks Until Christmas

"I'm sorry," my mom says.

She's sorry. She's fucking sorry.

It's yet another Christmas I'll spend alone.

This is why I hate this holiday. Every year, I get my hopes up that things will be different. Every year, I'm disappointed when I fall into the same goddamn trap.

"It's fine," I lie. "I have practice on Christmas Day anyway. I have to go."

I hang up without saying anything else. We're not really close enough for more words anyway. This was her obligatory annual call to let me know she's not coming to Vegas for Christmas.

I don't particularly want to spend the holiday with my family anyway. I've come in second with them my entire life, and getting together with them is a reminder that even in my personal life, I'm never first to anybody.

I made it all the way to the goddamn NFL, and I get to come in second as tight end number two. Or three, depending on the day and how well Chase Morgan is executing.

When Ben Olson retired, it was *finally* my turn. I was *finally* going to be the sole starting tight end for the Vegas Aces. Sure, I start games, but the Aces have traditionally run an offense that only required one on the field at a time. This was it. My shot. Fucking finally.

And then a new head coach brought in his baby brother to start over me, and I'm back to being second best.

It's the goddamn story of my life.

You'd think the glory of getting drafted and being good enough to get a spot on the fifty-three man roster would be enough. It's not.

I have fought tooth and nail to get where I am, and for what?

To sit out half the plays. To be a bystander. To watch someone else get to execute when I can't. To sub in when the starter gets tired or when our team is so far ahead it won't matter if I fuck it all up.

My competitive edge is starting to wear thin. I've resorted to devious tactics I'm not proud of to try to get ahead, and somehow even *that* has bitten me in the ass every damn time.

Every goddamn time.

I think it stems back to when I was five. I barely remember it, but it's a feeling I associate with my childhood. My parents decided to divorce, and I found out on Christmas Day. They were whisper-yelling at each other in the hallway, and I heard every word.

I was their only kid. My dad left, and I don't really know what happened to him. He just disappeared one day. My mom said he died a few years later, and my mom remarried. She had a kid with her new husband, and I was the third wheel. I was there because my mom didn't have anywhere else to send me.

It's why I turned to football. I found a family there—a brotherhood—a place where I fit in when it felt like I didn't fit in with my own family.

And now she's choosing my half-brother over me. Again. As usual. She's going to New York for Christmas to spend time with Carson, his wife, Tamryn, and their kid.

My mom hasn't been out to meet Mia. She'll be a year old in a month and a half, and her grandmother hasn't met her yet. At least her grandmother on my side hasn't.

Her grandmother on Kelly's side is pretty dope.

But my mom? She hasn't been to a single game this season. *Let me know when you're starting. I'll come then.*

I guess *starting* is the only way to make her proud. I officially give up.

She lives in Florida, where I grew up. Geographically, New York is closer to her than Vegas.

But she's made the same choice every year. Geography doesn't matter. I'm still second best to Carson. I'll always be second best to Carson, to starting tight end Asher Nash…fuck, even to whatever idea Kelly has in her head about me that's stopping her from being with me.

I'd love to figure out some way to get out of the rut I find myself in. It feels like I'm very nearly at rock bottom, which sounds so ridiculous as an NFL star who seems to have everything from the outside.

I don't. I don't have anything at all…except for my baby girl.

She's the one bright spot in an otherwise gray world. She's what keeps me going. She's my motivation to keep fighting, to work harder…to show her mother that I'm not the same guy who sold a video of my teammate to the highest bidder because of my grudge against his whole family.

I get it. It was a stupid decision that hurt her best friend since she's married to that teammate—or former teammate now, anyway.

13

But goddamn, she's been holding onto that grudge for a long time now. It's been a year and a half, and we tried reigniting things on and off when she was pregnant and after Mia was born.

During the time she was pregnant, I did another stupid thing when I bribed Terry Lawrence to be extra tough on Asher during practice. I caught hell for it, but it didn't stop me from doing other things to sabotage my teammates.

"Accidentally" bumping into players during practice to make them look unprepared and unreliable, "forgetting" to share important notes, making weak blocks when I knew it would cause someone else to take a hit—yeah, I've done all those things.

But they haven't garnered me the starting position. Instead, they've cost me my reputation in the locker room. That family I found through football? They've scattered, much like the family I'm related to by blood.

Everything was easier a few years ago—back before Lincoln Nash was named the head coach of the Vegas Aces. I was one of the crew. We were all members of the same exclusive *private* club, and then shit hit the fan when a list of members was released to the public. The club survived somehow, but it's not like it used to be.

And then Kelly found out I was still a member after we'd been seeing each other a while. Combined with her somehow knowing everything I've done, I guess she determined I'm not mature enough for her liking.

But ever since Mia was born, I've started fighting harder.

I want to be someone my daughter can be proud of someday, and to me, that means being a starter.

It also meant withdrawing my membership at the club, though it hasn't come up with Kelly since I left.

We all slip up sometimes. We take advantage of situations when we see ways they'll benefit us. It's not right, but it's the example my mother led by, and it's all I've ever known.

As I stare down at a picture of my little girl on my phone's lock screen, I realize how very badly I want to break the cycle. I don't want Mia to be like me, and maybe it's for the best for her to only get to see me once a week.

But I want more. I wish I could have more. The thought of coming in second to Mia—to some other guy her mother starts seeing who might get more time with her than I do—tears me apart. It claws at me and hurts like the worst sort of pain I've ever known.

But her mother *isn't* seeing anyone right now, so I'm holding onto hope that someday she'll change her mind about me.

Maybe that means changing who *I* am, too. Maybe it means stepping up the way Kelly would want me to.

And as for Christmas, well…I guess, apart from dropping off a gift for my daughter, it'll just be another day of the week for me.

I head to the Complex, the practice facility for the Vegas Aces, and I hit the weight room ahead of practice. I spot a few of my teammates in the locker room, but I can't say I'm particularly close to most of them anymore. I used to be close to some of the wide receivers. So close that we even had a crew that got together every week for drinks. But they're married now with families, so the Thursday Night Crew has changed.

I'm on the outside now, even though I have a kid now, too.

I pulled too many stunts for them to trust me, and it's easier for them to keep their tight bond and write me out of it.

I'd say I'm probably closest to the two tight ends who aren't related to the coach, and that's about it. I mainly keep to myself, and I feel every inch of that as I walk into a lonely locker room on a Saturday ahead of game day.

It's all part of that feeling of rock bottom. I wonder if getting out of Vegas would be any better, but trying to go somewhere else would take me away from my daughter. I'm already short on time with her. I don't know how I'd handle living in a different state entirely.

But you know what they say about rock bottom. There's only one way to go.

Chapter 3
Kelly Kaplan

Baby's First Christmas

Four Weeks Until Christmas

I hold up the little knit gingerbread man sweater that just arrived, and I feel a warmth inside my chest. I check the matching one I bought for myself, too, and they're a perfect match for my little mini-me and myself. I can't wait to take a photo of the two of us wearing them in front of our tree.

In fact, maybe it'll be the start of a new tradition. All the things we do this year will be the start of new traditions since it's Mia's first Christmas, and I pull the other clothes I ordered out of the box. The *Baby's First Christmas* onesie is even cuter in person than it was online, and a heat presses behind my eyes as I think about it.

There's just something so magical to me about Christmas, and I want to give Mia every inch of that magic each year the way my parents did for me. The torch has been passed to me, and I can't wait to give her the same experiences I had.

I always woke up on Christmas morning at my grandparents' house, and my parents assured me that Santa had left my presents under the tree back home. And they were right. I have no idea how he did it, but Santa always managed to visit our house while we were away, and there was nothing more exciting to a seven- or eight-year-old girl than to get home after visiting my grandparents for Christmas so I could check under the tree.

Oh, who am I kidding? I still checked it when I was fourteen or fifteen.

I'd still check it today if I still lived with my parents, to be honest.

But once I moved to Vegas, all that changed. I still head to Chicago for the holidays, but I don't get to go to Louisiana with my parents once they go back home anymore.

My real Christmas wish this year is for my parents to finally tell me they're going to move to Vegas…but somehow that seems like a dream that doesn't have a real chance of coming true. My mom is retired, but my dad is not. He's an executive for a telecommunications company—the same company that moved my parents from the suburbs of Chicago to Louisiana before I was born—and I know he wants to work until he's sixty-three for retirement purposes. He still has a couple more years.

Still, a girl can dream of her parents moving closer to her, right? My mom has told me *maybe* a few times, so I hang my hopes on that.

Speaking of my mom, I give her a call once I get home from work.

"Hey Kel," she answers. "How's the cookie business?"

I laugh. "As delicious as always. How are you two doing?"

"We are *so* excited to see that sweet baby for Christmas. And you, of course. Are you all set with your flight?"

"Yes. Thank you for the points to book it. I only bought one seat, just so you know," I say.

"Oh, honey, I told you that you could've gotten one for Mia," she scolds.

"It'll be fine, and I wanted to save you the points so you can visit me more often. Besides, nearly four hours of holding my sweet baby? It sounds like a treat, to be honest," I say.

"You sound like a new mom," she says, and it's probably because I *am* a new mom. Well, new-*ish*. She's not even a year old yet, and everyone tells me to soak in every moment while she's little, so I'm trying to heed that advice.

"Is it okay if I ship some gifts directly to Grandma?" I ask.

"Of course. Just let her know when to expect them and she'll probably even wrap them up for you, knowing her," she says.

My mom is an amazing mom, and it's because her mom was an amazing mom. I have lots of strong women to look to as good examples, and I'm blessed with strong, kind men, too.

And then there's Austin. He's strong, for sure. Kind? Not so much. I have such conflicting feelings for him because I *want* to be able to make things work with him, but our timing is always just…off.

I'm struggling to feel the sorts of things I felt for him with anyone else. I haven't been with anybody since I was last with him, and in part, it's because I'm a busy, single mom. But the other half is because there's just no one else who compares.

Maybe this Max dude will be the answer.

"I'm going on a date," I blurt.

"You are?" she asks. "With who? Please say Aus—"

"Not Austin," I say, cutting her off. I know she likes Austin, but she likes what she knows of him—the hot guy she watches in a football uniform on her television on Sundays who's a great daddy to her granddaughter. I left out some of the more devious things he's done. I didn't see any reason to tarnish his reputation with her, and I guess part of me is still hopeful he'll change those things. But do people ever really change? "This woman who frequents the bakery is setting me up on a blind date with her grandson."

"That's lovely, honey. I hope you have a great time," she says. I hear the disappointment in her voice.

I sigh. "I know you don't mean that."

"Of course I want you to have a great time." She sniffs a little defensively.

"But just with Austin, not with Max."

"Max? His name is Max?" she asks, and before she can say something like *isn't that a dog's name*, I jump in.

"He sounds really great," I lie. I don't know the first thing about him other than the fact that Mrs. Howard thinks we'd be perfect together, and his name is Max.

I set that aside for now. "Can we talk about Christmas traditions?" I ask.

"Of course."

"I want to start some new things for Mia, and I have about a million ideas and zero clue how realistic any of them are," I say.

We launch into a conversation about decorating Christmas trees and drinking hot cocoa and listening to Christmas songs and buying matching ugly Christmas sweaters, and I push aside that weird feeling in my chest.

You know…that strange feeling that maybe Austin would fit right into the picture even better than I could dream. My parents already love him. My daughter worships him.

I think I love him, too.

But I just don't know if I can trust that he won't hurt the people I care about…or me. And that's a risky gamble to take when it comes to my heart.

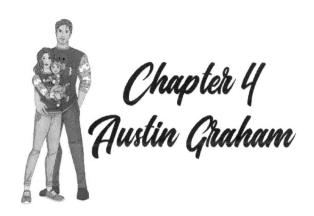

Chapter 4
Austin Graham

Winter Wonderland

Four Weeks Until Christmas

I feel pulled in ten different directions, and now that the season of giving is upon us, I feel even less enthusiastic than usual.

I just want to be alone, which is a difficult feat given my profession. I can isolate myself with my headphones in the locker room or the weight room to give off the vibe that I don't want to be bothered, but that's only going to cause further division between my teammates and me.

It's the stupid event I have to attend tonight that's causing me to feel this way. It's a charity Christmas party that I knew was coming but didn't have on my calendar, and I tried to get out of it, but our offensive coordinator says that if we can build bonds outside of the locker room, our chemistry on the field will be more electric.

It sounds like a load of hot shit to me, but I do what my coaches tell me to do, and since the entire coaching staff and most of the offense will be here, I'm sort of stuck.

Sometimes it feels like Coach Dixon decided to take me on as his pet project this season. Last season, he left me alone, but this season, he's up in my face all day, every day.

Which is why I was basically forced to cancel my night with Mia to attend this shindig that I don't want to be at.

At least I get to see Mia on Friday…and Kelly. Knowing that I'm going to see the two of them is my motivation. They always brighten everything around me when we're together, though Kelly seems to be pulling further and further away from me lately.

All things that contribute to my sour mood, I guess.

And as I slip into the suit I reserve for these events and attempt to tie the tie that no father ever taught me how to do my goddamn self, I find that sour mood worsening.

I blow out a breath as I glance at myself in the mirror. I throw a little extra gel in my hair before I head out the door.

I should've taken an Uber to this event instead of driving myself. At least then I could've had a few drinks to try to loosen up.

Instead, I clench my jaw as I pull up to the valet station. I get out of the car and hear the joyous Christmas music pumping from inside, and I find myself halting on the sidewalk outside of the event.

Dean Martin is singing about a "Winter Wonderland," but we're out here in the desert.

It's honestly one of the things I love about living in Vegas. No snow. No stupid white Christmas. No blizzards to battle, no ice to chip off my windshield, no slush in the streets.

So why even bother playing the music? Even as I have the thought, the song ends and "Let It Snow" begins.

I can't take it.

I'm about to turn around to get back into my car and call it a night when Coach Dixon gets out of the car behind me, followed by none other than Asher Nash.

Fuck, this is going to be a long night.

Asher has been putting in the work to bond with everyone in the locker room—except for me. There's a little bit of bad blood between us because of the history between his family and me. It feels like they're all out to get me, if I'm being honest.

And now he's engaged to Coach Dixon's daughter. It feels very much like these two are teaming up against me, even though that's likely not the case. They have no reason to team up against me.

Still, feeling like Dixon's pet project leaves a bad taste in my mouth. I get that he is a former tight end himself, so the position is important to him. I understand that he wants his teammates to bond, but I've bonded with everyone I'm interested in bonding with at this point.

Asher nods at me, and I give him the polite head nod of greeting back. I greet Coach Dixon, too, and then I turn to head inside before either of them can scoop me up into a conversation filled with mindless small talk—my least favorite of all kinds of talk, to be honest.

When I walk in, fake snow is coming out of machines perched all over the room, and it *is* a fucking winter wonderland with blankets of white polyester and cotton everywhere to mimic piles of snow.

Fuck it. I can take an Uber home and get my car tomorrow.

I beeline for the bar first.

Asher comes to a stop beside me at the bar. "Great, like I don't hear this type of music all day every day at home."

I think about last Tuesday when I went to pick up Mia, and Kelly was singing along with some channel playing Christmas songs. I think about replying with something about that, but before I get the chance, the bartender hands over my beer.

"You have a kid, right?" Asher says as I start to walk away.

I glance over at him and nod.

"A girl?"

I nod again. "Why?"

23

"My fiancée says Pampers are the best, but I like Huggies. Just curious what another dad thinks."

"We're a Kirkland household. There's nothing Kelly loves more than a trip to Costco...except maybe a trip to the craft store." I tilt my head a little. "Can I just say that never in a million years did I think I'd be bonding with Asher Nash over diapers?"

He laughs. "Feeling's mutual, man." It sort of feels like a breakthrough for us. He seems to be the kind of guy who sort of keeps to himself with his head down.

The same can't really be said for me. I've tried things from every angle—sucking up to coaches, playing my hardest, befriending people, becoming enemies with others. It just feels like no matter what I do, I can't win—especially not when the head coach is related to the tight end and the OC is his future father-in-law. That sort of fucks my chances from the word *go*.

Still, making this guy my enemy from the moment he walked in hasn't worked out all that well for me.

For the first time, I see the benefits of a potential friendship with Asher.

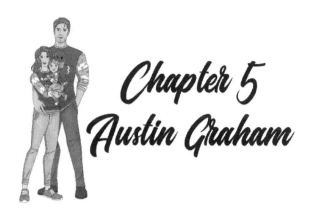

Chapter 5
Austin Graham

Less Grinch, More Elf

Three Weeks Until Christmas

When I get out onto the practice field, Coach Dixon is talking with my position coach. Ben Olson, a retired Aces player, is here, too, and he occasionally does consultations with the tight ends.

"Graham, Morgan, get over here," Coach Bruce barks at Chase and me. We both jog over because when your position coach calls you over, you fucking get your ass over there. "Dixon wants to run more two-tight-end formations, so one of you is going to start alongside Asher. I'll be watching you both, and I want to start with blocking and then see you running routes."

I glance over at Chase, and I hate that my first thought is how I can sabotage him.

I want this. I want it with everything inside of me.

But I want to earn it. No, I *need* to earn it.

I need to prove I'm the better player. I've done a few too many underhanded things, but it's time to start turning things around. This is my chance to prove I've changed.

I have to do this the right way—for Mia. For Kelly.

Chase doesn't have nearly as much to lose as I do.

So I get out onto the field and work my ass off to prove to Coach Bruce that I'm the one who deserves the starting position.

I fight like hell, and I'll do it again tomorrow.

"You coming, Graham?" Chase asks after practice.

I glance over at him. We often go out on Thursdays after practice as a way to self-soothe after the toughest practice of the week. I miss the old Thursday night crew. We used to have a hell of a fun time going to nightclubs or sex clubs or wherever the hell we wanted because we were a bunch of young, single pro football players.

The ladies didn't care that I wasn't a starter.

But then I met Kelly, and my life changed. My priorities changed. I didn't want to go out with the guys for drinks and pussy anymore. I just wanted to be with her.

I never wanted that before her.

But I managed to fuck it all up anyway. It's just what I do.

I shrug. "Sure."

"What about you, Nash?" Chase asks Asher.

He nods. "I'm in."

An hour later, I'm sitting in a booth with a beer in front of me. I'm with the other tight ends—Chase and Asher plus Justin Miller—when Justin and Chase excuse themselves to the bar to order another round.

That leaves Asher and me.

He clears his throat as he glances up at me. "Practice was good today. You think you got the edge over Morgan?"

I lift a shoulder. "I left everything out there that I had in me, so I guess it's up to Coach Bruce and Coach Dixon now."

He leans in. "Dixon likes you."

I raise my brows in surprise. I think about asking him how he knows that, but it's his girlfriend's dad. I suppose they talk shop even outside of business hours. "Thanks, man."

I'm not sure why the whole conversation leaves me feeling hopeful, but it does.

We have a light practice on Friday ahead of Sunday's matchup against the Ravens, and we're done by five. I worked my ass off this week proving myself, and at the end of practice, Coach Bruce pulls me aside.

"You're in."

It's two words that change my entire perspective on, well…everything.

I fought hard. I fought honestly.

And I won.

I almost *never* win that way…but I guess I also haven't really given it much of a chance.

I'll be starting alongside Asher this weekend.

My chest tightens as excitement courses through me.

I haven't been this excited about something in a long time.

Barring Mia, of course. And now, if I can just get her mother on board, we could really have it all.

I can't wait to tell Kelly that I'll be starting this week. I can't wait to play the little game of catch I've started playing with Mia when I have my time with her.

She sits on the floor, and I roll a soft, squishy pink football to her. She picks it up and tosses it anywhere but at me, and I lunge and stretch to try to catch it before it hits the floor as we both laugh and laugh.

I head straight for Kelly's place after practice. If anything, I'll get a little extra time with my daughter and her mother, and maybe we can celebrate together after we get Mia down for bed when I tell her how I earned this the right way—no sabotages, no advantages, no bribes.

Just honest to God hard work.

Maybe that'll be enough for her to see that I'm working hard to change. Maybe it'll be enough to win her back.

After all, becoming a starter is going to solve all my problems…right?

It's what I've always told myself, anyway.

When I ring the bell, I wait a full minute. No one answers. I suppose I'm a little early, though I never really said what time I'd be over—just *after practice*. Maybe I should've texted that I was on my way.

I try knocking, and a breathless Kelly throws open the door a minute later.

She's wearing a bathrobe, and her hair is tied up in a towel. If only I could slip her out of that bathrobe…

Her face is freshly scrubbed without makeup, and she's panting as she says, "You're early."

I can't help but think about how many times she's been beneath me panting.

It's been a while. Far too long, actually. We had a lot of fun last year and even a bit into this year after Mia was born, but it's been months.

Which means it's been *months* since I've been with anyone.

I used to play the field, and then I caught feelings for Kelly Kaplan.

And now…well, I'm holding out for her, I guess. I haven't had time to fuck around. When I have free time, I spend it with Mia. No other woman has caught my interest since I met Kelly, and I fucked up by not telling her that when I had the chance.

I fucked up by prioritizing myself over her.

I fucked up by hurting both her and the people she cares about.

I fucked up by losing her trust.

I'm hopeful that sharing my news with her will be the ticket to turning things around. I'm hoping she'll see that I'm changing for the better—that I'm earning things on my own merits and skills for a change.

I just want Kelly to see that I'm working hard to turn over a new leaf to be a better person—one Mia can look up to and respect.

"Sorry," I say as my eyes move up and down her robe. I don't bother hiding the fact that I'm checking her out and wishing I could touch what she has beneath the robe again. "Did I catch you in the shower?"

She nods and opens the door a little wider.

"Damn, I should've shown up a few minutes earlier." I smirk at her, and she rolls her eyes as I walk into the house.

She closes the door behind me, and I wander down the hall and into the family room, where I stop and take it all in.

The house looks like a winter wonderland, but this one doesn't give me those same feelings of disdain that I had at the charity event.

A beautiful Christmas tree sits in one corner with colored lights wrapped around it and ornaments sparkling and glowing. It reminds me of my childhood—of the Christmas I found out about my parents' divorce. Before the whispered fight in the hallway, the day was going well, and it's one of the few happy memories I have of my childhood before everything went to shit.

She has wreaths on the walls and garland along her mantle, and candles are lit as soft Christmas tunes play in the background. It's warm and comfortable in here, and for just a second, I wish we lived together. I wish I could wake up in this Christmas wonderland, that we could make love beside the tree while the baby sleeps in her room and when she wakes, we could go together and take her from her crib.

I have no Christmas decorations in my house. I always say it's because I don't have the time to put them up, but if I were really so inclined, I could hire someone to do it. I've just never been inclined.

Christmas is a happy occasion for some and filled with painful reminders for others. I guess I fall into the second category.

Call me a grinch, I guess. But Kelly, her house, and our daughter are the combination that makes me want to be less of a grinch and more of an elf.

"Mia's in the playpen in my bedroom," she says, interrupting my thoughts about Christmas. "I'll go **get her. How, uh...how late are you planning on hanging out? Or are you taking her somewhere?**"

"I was actually hoping we could all have dinner together tonight." I can't wait to tell her my news, but I didn't want to walk in and just blurt it out. I'm holding out for the right moment.

"Oh, I'm sorry, I can't." She twists her lips apologetically, and a little color rushes into her cheeks. "I, uh…I actually have a date tonight."

A…a date?

She's going on a *date*?

All the wind deflates from my sails, and at the same time, it feels like a punch to my gut.

"Oh," I say, and I don't bother hiding my disappointment.

"It's just a first date," she says, sort of backtracking a little defensively. "This sweet old lady from the bakery insisted I go out with her grandson. I don't even know what he looks like." She offers a nervous giggle, but I can't tell if she's nervous about the date or nervous to tell me about it. I hope it's the latter.

I clear my throat. It doesn't change the fact that she agreed to the date, and that pokes at me harder than I care for it to. "Oh," I say again, suddenly without words. "Well, uh, have fun, I guess."

"Thanks." She offers a tight smile. "I'll just go grab Mia for you."

She disappears into her bedroom, and I wish I could follow her, but I can't. It's not my place, and especially not when she's going on a date with someone else.

I haven't gone on a date with anyone else. How could she?

It's a clear reminder that she doesn't want me the way I still want her. She doesn't have the same **sorts of feelings for me that I have for her.**

It's a gut punch.

It should make me rethink my priorities. It should force me to move on.

But I don't want to. My priorities are Mia, Kelly, and football.

She returns a few seconds later with Mia, and I press my lips into a smile through the sadness I feel that her mother is going on a date tonight with another man. Maybe she'll fall in love with him. Maybe they'll get married.

Maybe Mia will call him *Dad* someday, too.

The thought breaks my heart.

I'm Dad. I don't want to share her with someone else. I don't want to share Kelly, either, but what the hell can I do?

Chapter 6
Kelly Kaplan

Vodka Shots in the Pantry

Three Weeks Until Christmas

I'm still in my bathrobe when I carry Mia out to Austin. "Dada!" she squeals when she sees him, and she reaches out of my arms for him.

She's a total daddy's girl. She *loves* him, and she loves spending time with him. Her first word wasn't *mama* even though I'm with her essentially twenty-four-seven.

It was *dada*. Dada gets *all* the glory while mama does *all* the hard work.

It warms my heart when I see them together, even though I'm trying to keep Austin at a distance.

But it's hard when I look into the blue eyes of my sweet baby and see the exact shade of Austin's. His dark hair is trimmed short, but he told me once that he had dark curls when he was little that looked exactly like Mia's.

My chest twinges a little as I hand her over—just like it always does. To be honest, I'm not sure if it's a twinge or an errant butterfly, but I do what I always do, and I push it away.

God, though. The way he looks when he's holding her, and the way he looks down at her...sometimes it's enough to make me feel ready to give it another try.

I was smitten with him from the very beginning, and before he did all the stupid things he thought would get him ahead, we actually had a lot of fun together.

I think because that's all it was. We were having fun. Neither of us had any expectations, so there was no pressure, yet I found myself falling for him.

And then he went and released that stupid video that hurt both Ava and Grayson, and I don't care that it was nearly a year and a half ago at this point. You don't betray your teammates that way—or the best friend of your girlfriend. Situationship. Um...the mother of your child.

Ava has moved on, obviously. It didn't have the lasting effects he might've been hoping for since they're happily married now and running an entire bakery together.

But I haven't gotten over it. I tried to. Really. I even continued seeing him after Ava told me the reason he initially had an interest in me was to get closer to Grayson so he could find ways to hurt him.

But ultimately, I couldn't get past any of it. He hurts other people for fun, and he demolished my trust in him. I was heartbroken after my last relationship ended with broken trust, and I just can't go down that road again, no matter how attracted I am to him.

No matter how much my ovaries explode when I see him holding our baby.

No matter how much I want him to put another baby in me. Whoa.

Did that errant thought really just pop into my head a mere hour before a *date* is coming to pick me up?

I liked being pregnant, and I definitely want more kids someday.

Would pregnancy have been a better experience if I wasn't on shaky ground with the father? Absolutely.

And I wish I could get off that shaky ground.

I clear my throat as I force those thoughts from my head. "I'm just going to go finish getting dressed."

I head into the bedroom and choose a light pink dress that makes my brown eyes seem lighter, like they're glowing, and sets off my dark hair. I pair it with matching shoes—which happen to be three-inch heels, something I'm not exactly used to walking in—and I apply my makeup and curl my hair.

I'm ready to go with about fifteen minutes to spare. This is normally when I'd take a shot of vodka while I wait for my date to pick me up to try to squash those first date nerves, but I can't exactly do that with Austin out there watching my every move.

I switch to my date night purse and head out to the family room, and I see Austin playing Mia's favorite game—toss the ball anywhere but at me.

I smile as I look down at them, and Austin glances up at me before he looks back at the ball he just rolled back to Mia.

And then he does a double take.

His eyes slowly drift from my legs up to my hips, up to my chest, and up to my face. He lets out a low whistle. "Wow."

Mia chooses that exact moment to pick up the ball and toss it, and for once, she hits her target, smacking Austin right in the forehead with the soft, squishy, ball.

He snaps to attention, laughing as he shifts his glance down to his daughter, and she lets out the sweetest giggle.

"You got me!" he says merrily to her, and I swear, he is a different person when he's with Mia. He's the kind of person I could see myself ending up with, if I'm being honest. He's sweet and kind and fun.

Why the hell am I going on a date with another guy when *this* guy seems almost perfect for me?

Oh, right. Because he's decidedly *not* perfect, and I can't be another person he can step on to get to wherever it is he's going.

Maybe that's why I'm holding onto this anger so tightly. It's not just the trust issues I have, but it's the fact that it feels very much like he used me to get to my friends, and now he's stuck with me since he knocked me up.

I want to feel chosen because of who I am, not because of who my friends are. I want to feel seen and heard and loved. Is that really so much to ask?

And aside from that, I want to feel valued and cherished, and I want someone who isn't going to abandon me the way my ex did. I can't afford to be abandoned at this point because it isn't just me anymore. I have a little one to think about, too, and it's a new armor I wear as I head out on my first date with someone other than Austin since I gave birth.

It feels…weird.

It's strange to be going on a blind date, but Max is picking me up here soon, and I'm not as excited as I wish I was. I sort of feel like I'm going to throw up, to be honest, and I think vodka would really help with that.

I sneak over to my small walk-in pantry since Austin is occupied with Mia, and I grab the bottle of Tito's. I unscrew the cap and help myself to a swig.

"Can I have some?" a deep voice behind me asks, and I spin around guiltily as I practically choke on the vodka.

He chuckles when he sees my wide eyes, and I hand the bottle over.

He takes the cap from my other hand and screws it back on without taking a sip. "I was just kidding since I'm with Mia tonight. I'm more of a whiskey drinker, anyway." He sets the bottle on the shelf. "Why are you sneaking shots of vodka in the pantry?"

He doesn't move, and the pantry is pretty small for one person. There isn't much space between us, and I can smell his aftershave.

It's the same woodsy scent that drew me in the first time we met, and somehow it makes me feel at home.

So much so that I've taken to stockpiling the mahogany-teakwood-scented candles from Bath and Body Works because they remind me of him.

I tell myself it's for Mia, so she can smell her daddy even when he's not here. But the truth is that it's for me, too.

"I'm nervous," I admit.

"About your date? You shouldn't be. Whoever this douche is…he's lucky you're giving him the time of day."

Douche? We don't know if he's a douche or not yet, but the doorbell rings, so I guess that means we're about to find out.

I clear my throat. "Excuse me," I say, nodding toward the doorway of the pantry so he'll let me out.

He blocks my path another few seconds. "Do I have to?" he asks, his voice barely above a whisper.

I glance up, and our eyes lock. I can't make myself nod or say yes or even form a coherent thought when he's looking at me like that, so we just face off until he finally presses his lips together and moves out of the way.

But *damn*. That heat between us?

Hot. As. Hell.

Chapter 7
Kelly Kaplan

Stop Saying Cockshot

Three Weeks Until Christmas

I open the door and find my date standing there.

"Max?" I ask the cute guy standing in my doorway, and he nods.

He's about my age and a little on the more studious side in his sweater over a buttoned-up shirt and black frames resting on his nose—especially in a side-by-side comparison with Austin, the pro athlete. "You must be Kelly. Let me start by apologizing for my grandmother."

I laugh. "No need to. Come on in, and I'll just grab my purse."

He stands in the entryway as I rush through my small house to kiss Mia on the head. "Bye, Miamiga."

"Don't I get one?" Austin asks, and I purse my lips and give him a look as I grab my handbag off the counter.

"I won't be late," I say quietly.

"Don't go at all," he whispers, and he grabs my hand.

My chest tightens, and I can't help but wonder *why* I agreed to this date. My first instinct was to say no, but I wanted to send Austin the message that I'm moving on.

Whether or not I'm lying to him. Or myself.

I sigh as I pull my hand back. "Bye." I head down the hallway and join Max, who glances up the hallway in the direction I came from as if he's wondering whose voices those were, but I don't answer his unasked question.

I know his grandmother knows I'm a single mom, but I have no idea whether she shared that with him or not.

We get into his car, a Volkswagen SUV, and he starts driving toward a restaurant. "So, you work at Cookie's Cookies?" he asks.

I nod. "I'm the office manager there." I'm about to add that I used to teach kindergarten but quit when I had my daughter so I could be with her, but I leave all that out. For now. "What about you?"

"I'm in computer programming."

Well, that sounds…boring. But I don't say that.

"Do you like it?"

He nods. "It's all right. Pays the bills. What about you?"

"I like it. My best friend owns the bakery, so I get to work with her every day. We have a lot of fun."

"My grandma raves about the cakes there."

"I don't make them." I have no idea why I just said that. What a stupidly blunt reply to a compliment to my workplace. I don't even know how to backtrack out of that, and it's clear I'm out of practice when it comes to dating. I guess I'm also out of practice when it comes to having a conversation with another adult.

We sit in awkward silence until we pull up to the restaurant, an Italian place, and I could really use another shot of vodka. He navigates the parking lot twice for a spot, and I've never been here, but it must be really good based on how crowded the parking lot is.

I hope he made a reservation.

I follow him into the restaurant once he finally parks. I glance around. It's a cute restaurant, and it's all decked out in Christmas décor, with a tree in the waiting area and garland along the walls with strings of lights setting a romantic vibe. A live band is playing Christmas songs in one corner of the place, and people are yelling to have a conversation over the music.

Okay, Kaplan. Get your head in the game.

It's not a *great* first-date location, but we can make it work. I'm outgoing enough that I can make pretty much anything work, right? Time to dial up the sunshine and dial back whatever that was in the car. I'll attribute it to first-date nerves.

I hum along to "Winter Wonderland" as Max yells to the hostess.

"We have a reservation for two," he says.

"Sorry, it's so busy. We're hosting a company Christmas party, so it's a bit busier than normal. What name is the reservation under?" she asks.

"Max Cockshot," he yells just as the song ends.

Oh dear.

Everyone turns and looks at him…or at least it feels that way. Cockshot?

Wait a minute. Max Cockshot? As in…*maximum* Cockshot?

Wow. His parents didn't do him any favors. I'm scared to ask what his middle name is.

Kelly Cockshot. If this works out, I might have to keep my maiden name.

"I'm not seeing a reservation for Cockshot," the hostess says. "Hmm, Cockshot, Cockshot, Cockshot."

Oh my God. It takes *everything* inside me not to burst into laughter every time she says the name, and I can't help but think what Austin would say about this whole situation.

No! Get him out of your head! You're out with someone else. You're moving on.

Except, clearly, I'm not.

"Oh! There you are, next Friday night for two." She glances up at us, and we look at the rather long line of people waiting to be seated.

"There must be some mistake," Max begins.

"So sorry, but you're down for next week, Mr. Cockshot. If you want, you can find a spot in the bar. They serve food in there, too."

He glances at me, and I nod. I just need her to stop saying Cockshot.

We head toward the bar, which is packed full of people, but Max seems to eagle-eye spot a seat opening by the bar, and he swoops in gracefully to snag it for me. It's just one stool, so we can't sit together. I order a Tito's with soda, and he orders a glass of red wine as he stands behind me. It's not a real conducive setup for chatting, so I try to half-turn in my seat so we can talk.

"So, you're the office manager, and you don't bake. What else do you do at the bakery?" he asks.

"Manage the books, manage the phones, keep the schedule. All sorts of things. But what I really love is—"

We're interrupted when Max looks away from me and up at the bartender, who drops off some menus for us as our drinks are prepared.

I was going to talk about my hobby of making wreaths that my best friend was able to incorporate into my job as I make decorations for the bakery, but the moment is interrupted as Max grabs a menu and flips it open to study it carefully.

I study mine, too. I actually study it *hard* to find something that I can eat *fast*. Maybe I can just Uber it home early. It feels like this date is tanking fast, and I don't care quite enough to save it.

The bartender places our drinks in front of us, and I order a club sandwich. I don't pay much attention to what he orders.

I grab my drink just to have something to keep my hands and mouth busy, and even as I think it, I think of Austin telling me he has something that would keep my mouth and hands busy…but why the hell am I thinking about Austin when I'm on a date with Max? Max Cockshot.

Mr. Cockshot reaches for his glass of wine just as someone bumps into his arm, and…yep, you guessed it.

The red wine goes flying. It spills all over the bar and drips down onto me…all over my favorite pale pink dress.

I close my eyes with a heavy sigh as he grabs a napkin and starts rubbing the stain in even worse toward the bottom of my dress.

It's too late to save it. Red wine isn't coming out of this fabric. This dress is as good as done.

Either this is the start of a hilarious story we'll share with the future Cockshot kids one day, or there won't be a second date.

I'm guessing it's the latter.

At least it's a hilarious story I can share with Austin when I get back home.

Chapter 8
Kelly Kaplan

Dealbreaker

Three Weeks Until Christmas

He was sweet enough to walk me to my door, but then he tried for a kiss, as if I gave him any indication whatsoever that I was interested in *kissing* him after we barely even got to know a single thing about each other.

I pretended I didn't see him move in as I turned to unlock my front door, and I bid him goodnight before he could ask to have one more drink as a way to try to get into my pants—I mean into my *house*.

Yeah…no. Not happening, Cockshot.

I lean against the front door after I close it, and I draw in a deep breath.

The television is blaring a commercial in the next room, but I need a second to brush off that date.

If that's what's out there, I'm definitely not ready to move on. Whatever message I was trying to send to Austin doesn't matter. We definitely have some sort of situationship, and the fact that I couldn't stop thinking about him when I was out with Max tells me I never should've agreed to a date in the first place.

In fact…I think it might've done the opposite.

Austin Graham gives me tingles, and he's made enough passes at me for me to know he's still interested.

But I'm scared.

I know this is my trust issue speaking out, and that's something I have to deal with. But his track record is proven. As little as a few months ago, I found out he'd been working with a guy on defense to make life harder on Ava's brother-in-law, Asher.

The Nashes are as good as family to me, too, after the opportunities they've given me. Ava and Grayson took me in and gave me a healthy compensation package at the bakery, and I'm forever in their debt. So it was one more strike against Austin. One more reason not to trust him.

I shake the thoughts out of my head as the sounds of *Paw Patrol* in the family room register. Is Mia still awake? I glance at the clock hanging on the wall—it's only nine, but she should be asleep by now. Are they watching television together?

I push off the door and walk through the house, and that's when I spot them.

A father asleep on the reclining chair of the couch, his little girl perched on his chest—also asleep. His arms are holding her close, and his lips are planted on the top of her head as Chase barks about saving Santa on the television.

My heart swells in my chest as I stare at them.

It's possibly the most adorable scene I've ever witnessed in my life, and I quietly wrestle my phone out of my purse to take a picture of the two of them so I can stare at the sugary sweetness of it any time my heart desires.

I slip my phone back into my purse, and I locate the remote. I click the television off, and that's when Austin jolts a bit and comes to.

He doesn't dare move so as not to wake Mia, but his eyes move to mine. "Sorry," he mouths.

I can't help when a soft smile lifts my lips.

His eyes move down my dress. "What happened?" he whispers.

I chuckle. "Long story," I whisper back. I nod to Mia. "May I?"

He nods, and I lift her off of him and carry her to her bedroom. I kiss the top of her head and set her in her crib, and I sing a quick version of "Twinkle Twinkle Little Star." I feel sad I missed her falling asleep even though I know she was in good hands with her dad.

I'm startled when I turn and find him leaning on the doorway watching me.

I jump a bit, and he whispers another *sorry*.

I sneak past him, our arms brushing on my way by. "I'm just going to go change."

"Need any help?"

I press my lips together and eye him warily, and then I head to my bedroom.

I mean…it's not the *worst* idea, is it? I could just not change and walk back out to the family room naked.

I don't.

I slip on a pair of pink fleece reindeer pajama pants and a green Santa shirt, and I'm about as unsexy as it gets as I carry my dress in my hands to deposit it into the big garbage can in the kitchen.

He's sitting in the same seat where he was sleeping only moments ago, and he doesn't look like he's going to leave anytime soon.

I don't really want him to go.

I find myself not wanting him to go a little more each time he's here. Usually on Tuesdays, he takes Mia for the day, and he returns her after dinner time.

This is different.

It's something I feel like I could easily get used to, and part of me is trying to remember *why* that's a bad thing.

"So, what happened to the dress?" Austin asks.

I clear my throat. "My, uh...*date* knocked over a glass of wine, and my dress took the brunt of it." I shrug as I head to the garbage can and toss it in.

"How was the date?" he asks, and I hear the caution in his tone.

I walk over and plop down onto the couch beside him, and I set my feet on the table in front of me before I answer. "Safe to say there won't be another."

"Because he ruined your favorite dress?"

How'd he know it's my favorite?

Because I couldn't stop thinking about you.

I shake my head. "No chemistry."

He reaches over and squeezes my thigh a little. "Sorry. But honestly...yeah, no. I'm not sorry." He doesn't remove his hand, and the spot on my leg where his hand rests burns, as if all the nerves in my body are reacting to his touch and all the blood is rushing to the spot where his hand is.

I lean my head over onto his shoulder as I huff out a chuckle. "Plus, his last name is Cockshot."

"Deal-breaker."

"At least if I plan to change my name, it is."

"Are you?" he asks. "When you get married someday, I mean."

I lift a shoulder. "Probably."

Kelly Graham has a nice ring to it, not that I've thought about it. Or I did, I guess. Back when we were dating.

I straighten and glance over at him, and his eyes are burning into mine.

What changed?

It's like suddenly he's irresistible to me. I mean, sure, I've always liked him. I've always been interested. But I have the strangest urge to lean over and kiss him.

"Are you ready to give this another chance yet?" he asks quietly.

Heat burns between us.

I'm getting closer, but I'm too scared to admit that to him.

I give him my standard answer. "Not yet."

"It's getting late. I guess I should head home," he says, finally moving his hand from my leg and leaving a cold chill in its wake. He moves to stand, and I stand, too, so I can walk him out.

We head down the front hall, and I keep thinking I should come up with something—anything—to get him to stay, but I'm coming up short.

He stops when we get to the front door, and he sets his hand on the handle. Before he pushes it down to open the door, though, he turns back around to face me. "I had some news I wanted to share with you earlier."

My heart skips a beat at his words. Is he about to tell me he's seeing someone?

It surprises me that's the first thought that runs through my head, but there it is.

"What is it?" I ask, my voice hoarse as I wait with a bit of anxiety.

"I'm starting on Sunday," he blurts.

"Oh my God, Austin! Congratulations!" I squeal, and I toss my arms around his neck. I know how much he's wanted this. I know he's been working for it.

He laces an arm around my waist as I hug him, and I pull back but not out of his arms.

"And before you say anything, I want you to know I worked my ass off to make it happen. I didn't sabotage anyone, didn't bribe anyone. Just good, old-fashioned, hard work."

"I'm so proud of you," I say, my voice low.

His eyes flick to my lips. "I can get you a couple of tickets if you'd like to come."

"I'd love to."

He drops his head a few inches, and my heart thunders as his lips move to mine.

God, after all this time, he still affects me. Deeply. Wildly.

His lips brush across mine, and it's just the softest breeze of a kiss, but it's still a kiss.

He pulls back, letting me out of his embrace even though it's not really what I want, and he turns to open the door.

"Good job, Graham," I say, and I'm not sure if I'm talking about getting the chance to start, doing it the right way, or that kiss.

He turns back toward me, and he grins. "Back at you, Kaplan." He winks, and then he walks out the door.

I close it behind me, and I lean on it like I did not so long ago when I arrived home. Instead of doing it to compose myself after a not-so-great date, though, I do it to compose myself after that heated little exchange.

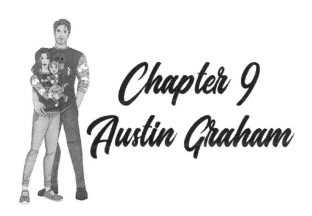

Chapter 9
Austin Graham

Put Me to Work

Two and a Half Weeks Until Christmas

We win on Sunday, and I fully believe it's because Kelly is in the crowd watching with her Graham forty-one jersey on.

I fully believe that's why I have the drive of competition in me. I'm fired up, and I score on the third play of the game only to glance up and see her screaming like crazy in the crowd. She catches me looking and waves at me, and I wave back to let her know I'm thinking of her even in the moments when I'm scoring a touchdown for my team.

How the fuck did that happen?

Better yet...*when* did that happen? I've always played for myself, but maybe that's because I never had anyone else to play for.

And maybe I do now.

Kelly found a babysitter and brought Ava to the game, and every time I looked up from the field into the stands, I saw the two of them laughing and having a great time.

Having her in my stadium, wearing my jersey, makes me feel a little less lonely.

It feels a little less like rock bottom today…like maybe she's here today for more than just supporting the father of her child. She's here because she wants to be.

At least…that's what I'm hoping.

When Tuesday rolls around, I head to Kelly's place to pick up Mia. It's Kelly's day off from the bakery, and when she answers the door, she looks…flustered.

"You okay?" I ask, reaching over to remove a piece of ribbon from her hair.

"Yeah, I'm fine. Good. I just…" She sighs. "Come on in."

I follow her into the family room, and she has a six-foot folding table set up with all sorts of crafting supplies on it. I spot Mia on the floor unspooling a roll of red and silver ribbon, and I walk over and grab it from her.

I respool it as I ask, "What's all this?"

"Mrs. Howard—the woman who set me up on that awful date last Friday—she told me she'd pay fifty bucks for one of the wreaths I made for the cookie shop. At the game on Sunday, Ava encouraged me to sell them at the shop, so I thought I'd use today for my side project and bust out a bunch of wreaths. Only…I can't really get anything done with this sweet little doodlebug here."

I chuckle as I watch that sweet little doodlebug lift herself to standing using the chair Kelly presumably was sitting on before she answered the door. Mia proceeds to run her hand along the top of the table, knocking all the decorations Kelly had organized on the top into disarray.

Kelly huffs out a sigh, and I swoop in and pick up Mia. Her shirt rides up a little, and I lift her into the air and blow raspberries on her stomach. She dissolves into giggles, and I tuck her into one arm like a football as I bend down to pick up all the things she just tossed on the floor.

"What can I do to help?" I ask.

She's staring at me with a touch of awe in her eyes, and she pushes her hair out of her face. "You're doing it."

I laugh. "No, really. I can help with more than just keeping Mia out of your hair."

"You know how to make wreaths?" she asks, narrowing her eyes at me.

"Well, no," I admit. "But I can help keep things organized, or you can teach me." I carry Mia over to her highchair, and I strap her in. I set the tray on top and pour some Cheerios onto the tray, and then I pull the highchair closer to Kelly's workstation.

I put *Paw Patrol* on the television since the pups always make Mia giggle even though I can't be sure she really understands what she's looking at, and then I head to the kitchen table to grab another chair. I set it beside Kelly's at the worktable. "Put me to work," I say as I sit beside her.

She raises her brows. "You sure?"

I nod, and she hands me a circular metal thing. She points to some greenery that looks like it came off a Christmas tree, and she hands me some wire.

"First step is to secure some wire to the ring. We attach the bigger greens in the back, and we layer in smaller bunches on top. So if you could make the base with a bunch of the big pieces, that would be a huge help to get me started."

I pretend like I understand everything she just said, and I start wrapping some wire around the metal ring. She watches me for a few seconds before she reaches over and guides my hands to show me how she does it.

Her hands are on mine, and for a second, it's like she doesn't realize it. But then her eyes shift to mine. Hands still touching, our eyes lock into some heated moment I don't ever want to step out of.

"Dadadada!" Mia calls, snapping us out of our trance.

I glance over at her as Kelly pulls her hands back and refocuses her attention on the wreath she's been working on. "Mimimimi," I say back to her, and she giggles as she tosses some Cheerios onto the floor.

"No, no," I say, shaking my head. "Cheerios go in the mouth, not on the floor. See?" I snatch one off her tray and pop it into my mouth.

She mimics me, popping one into her mouth too.

"You two are cute," Kelly says, and I glance over at her with a raised brow as I set my hand on my chest dramatically.

"Cute? Me?"

She laughs, and we get back to our tasks. She holds up the wreath she's been working on after a few minutes, and she eyes it. "Something's missing," she murmurs.

"Looks good to me," I say, inspecting it, but she drops it onto the table and shoves another bunch of greens onto one side before holding it up again.

"There." She sets it back down and starts laying out pinecones on top of it as if she's figuring out where she's going to set each one, and I continue wrapping the big pieces along the ring.

We work together as Mia snacks on her Cheerios, and eventually Kelly starts to make conversation.

"What are your plans for Christmas?"

"I don't really have any," I admit. "It's on a Thursday, so I'll have practice. You?"

"I'm going to Chicago. I always met my parents at my grandparents' place over Christmas break back when I was teaching, so it sort of feels like tradition now."

"Oh," I grunt. I don't mean to be short. If she wants to go to Chicago, she should. It's just…I was hoping to see Mia on Christmas at some point, particularly given that this is her first Christmas. I guess it's not all that important to me since the holiday is meaningless for me, but somewhere deep down, I was hoping to start a new tradition. I was hoping to find a way not to dread the holiday—to replace the bad memories with some new, good ones.

"If you don't want me to go—" she begins, but I interrupt her.

"No, not at all. You should go, especially if it's tradition." I bury the thought about wanting to see Mia.

"I figured if you had practice, you wouldn't mind."

I clear my throat. "Yeah. Absolutely. I'll be gone most of the day." I don't mention the fact that Lincoln Nash also has kids and will likely cut practice short depending on how we performed the week before and who our upcoming opponent is. Wednesdays and Thursdays are typically our two toughest days of practice in season, but if we put in enough work on Wednesday, we might go lighter on Thursday.

But it doesn't matter. I have no one to celebrate with.

Not even my own daughter.

I'm quietly introspective after that. I finally got the starting position, and…

Now what?

It didn't solve my problems.

Sure, we shared a kiss last Friday, but it didn't seem to get us anywhere. We didn't talk about it. She's still holding back, still doesn't trust me, still thinks I'm too immature.

So what else can I do to prove I've changed? Will there ever be *anything* that's enough, or is it time for me to finally just figure out some way to move on?

As I sit here wrapping wire around tree branches as my baby girl giggles happily in a highchair, and I sit beside this woman who I've fallen for over the last year and a half, I can't help but wish I had the answers to those questions.

Chapter 10
Kelly Kaplan

Sorry

Two and a Half Weeks Until Christmas

I glance at the clock when I hear Mia's cry as she wakes from her nap, and I realize it's well past lunchtime.

We've been making wreaths for the last three hours, and he's been an absolute godsend of help when I wasn't expecting it at all. He's been making all my bases and taking care of Mia in between, even putting her down for her nap, and we've knocked out four entire wreaths and started two more.

We make a pretty damn good team, as it turns out.

"Did you want to grab some lunch?" I ask.

"I'm full from all the Cheerios, but sure," he says with a laugh.

"Want to come with me to drop these four wreaths at the bakery? We could just grab lunch there. The chicken salad on French bread is to die for." I close my eyes and lick my lips as I think about how good the sandwiches Ava added to the lunch menu are, and when I open my eyes, I watch as Austin visibly adjusts himself.

Something clicks as his eyes meet mine.

57

Wait a minute…

Is he *affected* by me?

And am I really that clueless?

I mean…sure, he's been flirting with me, but I thought that was just his whole personality. The way he's looking at me, the way he dropped everything today to help me, the way he kissed me the other night—it all adds up to *feelings*, and for as much as he's flirted and asked over the last year, I thought he just wanted to mess around. Sex. Friends with benefits, or *coparents* with benefits…whatever.

But this right here *feels* different, and I'm not sure how I'm supposed to categorize that.

I tear my eyes away from him. "I'll just go get Mia changed and ready to go," I say hurriedly, and I rush out of the room before I say something I regret.

I'm not sure what I might say apart from *kiss me*, but I'm not going to say that. Right now. At least I don't think so.

This isn't uncharted territory, obviously. We share a child. But it *feels* new and different, and I'm not sure what changed.

I know he's been working hard to earn the starting position, and maybe that flipped a switch in him. He's been so busy competing on the field that he hasn't given his personal life much thought, and now that he's reached one goal, he can focus on something else.

It's either that or I'm reading *way* too much into things. Probably that. I need to get my head on straight. Maybe it's just the holidays and the stress of getting these wreaths done that are playing games with me.

Mia is all smiles as I walk into her bedroom to pick her up out of her crib, and she starts with the *dadadada* stuff. I smile, and she points behind me.

I turn around and spot Austin standing in the doorway. He's grinning at the two of us as he sweeps into the room and stands beside me.

Could we really have it all? Could this be a normal Tuesday for us, with him off work and the two of us working together for a common goal as we get the baby from the crib and head out for a lunch date?

Maybe we could, but then I think about where we're going: Ava and Grayson's bakery. My close friends. The ones who have given so much to me.

Could I really repay their debt by being with someone who acted with malicious intent against them?

It's always that nagging thought in the back of my mind that stops me short from pursuing things with him…no matter how much I want to ignore that voice.

He volunteers to drive, and he carries the wreaths out to his car and buckles Mia into the car seat before slipping into the driver's seat of his Escalade. It's quiet as he starts the car, and I've noticed that about him. He almost never has music on as he drives, and I finally ask him about it.

"How come you never listen to music?"

"I always listen to music. I just flip it off when I get out of the car and don't turn it on when I have a guest in the car."

"Why not?"

He lifts a shoulder. "Conversation."

He's quiet as he backs out of my driveway.

"What do you want to converse about?" I ask.

He chuckles. "Have you figured out your price point on your wreaths?"

"Mrs. Howard said she'd pay fifty, so I was thinking forty, actually. I think she was just being nice."

"You want my opinion?" he asks.

I glance at him, a little nervous for what he's about to say. "I'm not sure. Do I?"

He nods. "Yeah. You do. You're selling yourself short at fifty. I did a quick search earlier and found most handmade wreaths like yours going for over a hundred bucks."

"Yeah, but those are by pros. It's just a hobby for me." I lift a shoulder.

"Yours look better than most I saw online, Kel. Take into account your materials and your time, plus the fact that you had a professional football player helping you...I think you should charge at least one twenty-five. Take orders for a little personalization, and you could up that to one fifty."

I wrinkle my nose. "You're nuts."

"I'm dead serious. Try it." He glances quickly at me before his eyes return to the road.

"I don't know. I don't think I could take putting them in the shop and nobody even looking at them because of the price tag."

"You're in charge, so you decide. But that's my two cents."

I consider it as he finds a parking spot. Maybe I'll ask Ava for her opinion. She knows the clientele better than I do, and it's not like her cookies are free.

Austin grabs the stroller from the trunk and sets it up while I grab the wreaths, and he straps Mia in. We walk toward the bakery, and I'm glad I have the employee badge as we walk up and see a line out the door for the lunch rush. I head to my office with Austin right behind me, and I set the wreaths on my desk.

Ava appears in my doorway a minute later, and she eyes Austin without any judgment crossing her eyes before she turns to me. "What are you doing here on your day off?"

I nod toward the stack of wreaths. "I finished a few, and I was raving about the chicken salad, so we're here for lunch."

"Oh, they turned out *so* cute, Kel!" She walks over and picks one up. "How much? I want one for my house."

"Take one. They're free for you."

She makes a face at me that says *no way, absolutely not, I won't hear of it.*

"I told her to charge one twenty-five," Austin says. "Similar ones online go for that, but she was only going to charge fifty. What do you think?"

"I say go for it. If no one takes it for one twenty-five, you can always lower it," Ava says.

I look back and forth between the two of them, kind of surprised they're ganging up on me over price. I finally blow out a breath. "Fine. Ninety-nine ninety-nine."

Ava grins. "Save the one with all the red for me. I'll grab two sandwiches for you. Anything for Mia?"

I shake my head and pull a little lunchbox out of my purse. "I've got hers right here, but she wouldn't say no to one of your sugar cookies."

She grins. "Coming right up, along with a Pepsi and a bag of Doritos. Can I get you anything else, Austin?"

He looks surprised that she addressed him. "I'll take a Pepsi and Doritos, too."

She smiles. "You got it."

"Deduct the total from a hundred," I call after her as she turns to leave.

"Pfft," she says with an eyeroll. I didn't come here for a free lunch, but clearly that's what I'm getting. Plus enough money to pay for tons of new supplies to make more wreaths.

Grayson is the one who brings the food to my office. We've got Mia set up in the highchair we keep in here, and Austin's sitting across from me while I create price tags for the wreaths.

"Graham," Grayson says to Austin, and he nods cordially.

"I'll take those out and hang them up now," Grayson says, nodding to the wreaths.

"Before you go," Austin says, standing. "Can I talk to you a second? Ava, too, if she has the time."

Grayson's brows pinch together, but he nods. "Let me grab her."

I glance over at Austin, but his eyes won't meet mine, and a nervous tingle shoots up my spine over what he's doing.

"What's going on?" I ask, standing.

"You'll see."

61

Ava and Grayson appear in the doorway a minute later, and Austin walks over toward them. He turns back to me, and our eyes lock as he draws in a deep breath. He nods a little before he turns back to my best friend and her husband.

And then he says the words that actually shock me to my core. "I'm sorry. You two didn't deserve what I did to you, and I know it was a long time ago, but I realized recently that I never apologized to you."

"Thank you, Austin," Ava says quietly.

"We appreciate it, man," Grayson says, slapping him on the back. "Consider it water under the bridge."

"Thanks," he mutters. "And your brother, too—well, both of them. Coach and Asher. I'll talk to the two of them separately, but I want you to know that I'm deeply sorry for all of my actions against your family. I'd like to set a better example for my daughter than the one that was set for me, and it feels like the right time to start."

I feel heat pinching behind my eyes at his words.

"Asher actually just walked in a few minutes ago if you want to talk to him," Grayson says. "He's in the kitchen grabbing lunch." He motions with his head in that direction, and Austin follows him out there.

Ava stands in the doorway, and her jaw is slightly open in surprise. I must look the exact same way. "Whoa. I did not have *Austin apologizes* on my bingo card for today."

I can't help a small laugh. "Neither did I, to be honest. It seems like he's really trying to change."

She presses her lips together and nods. "It does. And to be perfectly honest, Grayson and I both forgave him ages ago. You know how boys are. They beat each other up, avoided each other a while, and then they were fine after that." She clears her throat as her eyes move to me pointedly. "I think maybe it's time for you to do the same."

I nod. "Yeah. Maybe. But I'm scared."

She walks toward me and gives me a quick hug before she pulls back and holds me by my upper arms. "Of course you are. But that's only because you feel so deeply for him. I see it, Kel, and I want you to have the best. And maybe that really is Austin." She lets go of my arms as she shrugs a little. "God, I never thought I'd say that, but I think it's *you*. I think he *says* he wants to be better for Mia, but really he wants to be better for both of you."

I give her a wary look.

"I'm serious. I see the way he looks at you, and…" She shakes her head. "I don't know. I think he wants the same thing you do, and I think…why not? You're always going to be afraid of getting hurt since you *have* been hurt, so why not jump in headfirst and see where it takes you? What if you *don't* get hurt this time but instead you get everything you want? Besides, it's Christmas. It's the time of forgiveness."

"Isn't that technically Easter?"

"Whatever. There's never a bad time to let go of the past and give someone a fresh start."

The men walk back into the office before I get the chance to reply, but she's definitely given me some food for thought.

Chapter 11
Austin Graham

Reindeer Pajama Pants

Two Weeks Until Christmas

Me: *Are you still awake?*

If she isn't and my text just woke her up, well, I'll feel like an asshole.

But the plane just touched down after I spent a lot of the ride talking with Asher, and we'll take a bus back to the Complex, where we've all parked our cars, and then we go home.

Only...I don't want to go home to my empty house.

I want to go to Kelly's house. I want to *be* with her.

She's all I've thought about since Tuesday. It was just a routine, mundane day. We spent the morning making wreaths. We went to lunch. I dropped her back at her place and took Mia to my place for a few hours to give Kelly some time to herself.

When I dropped Mia back off, I didn't want to leave.

I never want to leave the two of them, but the pull to stay was stronger than it has been the last few months.

Some dynamic is changing between us, and I'm not sure what it is or why. It's the long, lingering glances and the little touches.

It's these small things that feel exciting again, as if we're at the start of something new.

Only…it's not new. Not totally, anyway. It just *feels* new.

And because of that, there's nobody I want to share today's victory with more than her.

Typically we win, and I head home and sulk—not because we won, but because I didn't feel like I did all that much to contribute to that victory. In general, I don't leave games in a good mood. In general, I don't go through *life* in a good mood.

But Kelly's changing all that.

Starting is changing all that, too. It's all coming together at the same time for me, just like I knew it would when I got the starting position.

Tonight, I *did* contribute to the game. I was part of our victory rather than part of the sidelines.

I was on the field for fifty-six out of sixty-four snaps tonight. I blocked the hell out of the defensive back on the other side of the ball. I created running lanes for Jaxon Bryant, I caught the ball on the plays where I was supposed to run a route, and I scored a touchdown—my third of the season now.

Kelly: *Yes. Congrats on a great game! Mia and I watched.*

Me: *Thank you. Can I swing by?*

Kelly: *Now?*

Me: *[laugh emoji] Yes, now.*

Kelly: *I'm in my pajamas.*

Me: *Please tell me tonight's choice is that tight, see-through white T-shirt with no shorts.*

It was her preferred sleepwear when we were sleeping together, and every time I picture her sweet little body in that getup, my cock immediately swells. Like right now.

Kelly: *Even better. Reindeer pajama pants with a long-sleeve T-shirt.*

I laugh out loud.

Me: *On my way.*

She wasn't lying. When she opens the door, she's in pink reindeer pants and a matching shirt. "What's going on?" She leans on the doorframe as I stand on her front porch, the outdoor light beside her front door shining in my eye like a spotlight and making me feel like I'm on some sort of stage.

I stare at her as I realize...I have no plan.

There's no *reason* I'm here other than the fact that I wanted to see her. And so, in the same vein as proving I'm not the same immature asshole who hurt the people she loves, I decide to go for honesty.

"I wanted to see you."

She looks a little taken aback by that. "Oh. Why?"

I clear my throat, and I nod to her front hall. "Can I come in?"

She pushes off the door frame and holds out an arm. "You did great today, Austin. That play in the second quarter, it was—"

I cut her off as I loop an arm around her waist and haul her into me. I stare down at her as I try to figure out my next move.

"The baby's already asleep," she says quietly. "What are you doing here?"

"I told you. I wanted to see you."

Her breath hitches as her eyes search mine, and I can't help myself. I lean down and press my lips to hers for just a brief moment, and then I lift her into my arms and twirl her into a circle.

She laughs as I set her down. "What's gotten into you?"

"I'm in love with you, Kelly." The words just fall out of me unexpectedly, but I don't regret them.

In fact, far from it. I'm *glad* I said it. I've been thinking it for weeks, maybe even months, and it feels like a weight off my shoulders to voice the words aloud.

A soft gasp falls from her lips.

"I haven't stopped thinking about you since the last time I saw you. I don't want to only see you once a week. I don't want to be two passing ships. I don't want to only get time with our daughter when I'm picking her up and dropping her off. I want you. I want a life with you. Both of you. I want you to see how hard I'm working to be a man who's worthy of you even though I know I'll never deserve you or that sweet little girl. I—"

My last sentence is swallowed as her lips slam to mine. She presses her body fully against me, and I walk with her in my arms until her back is against the wall. I open my mouth to hers, and our tongues battle together in this expression of feelings that I've been burying for far, far too long. She moans as she sinks into me, and that's it. That's the signal.

We've been together enough times for me to know what that little moan means. She wants this, too. She's as tired of fighting it as I am.

I'm not here to fight anymore. I'm here to finally, *finally* get back on the same page with her.

She links her arms around my neck, her fingertips reaching into my hair as I deepen our kiss, my tongue exploring her mouth as if I've never explored it before—as if my cock hasn't been in her mouth, in her cunt, in her ass.

I want to take every part of her again, and I want us to be free of all the shit that's been hanging over us for two years.

And just when I think it's going to happen, she pulls back. Her eyes are hazy with lust, but she seems to come to a decision in the moment.

"Austin, I—I can't. You know where I am on us."

"I know," I say softly. I lean my forehead down to hers as I draw in a deep breath. "I know. I just…I guess I was hoping you could get to where I am."

"Which is where?" she asks.

I pull back a little, but not out of her arms. "With you. Figuring out a way we can be together—for us. For her." I lift a shoulder as I nod into the house toward Mia's room, the vulnerability not at all like me.

She glances down the hall, and I can see her resolve cracking.

I shake my head, and this time I do back up out of her arms. "It's okay. I don't want to pressure you into something you don't want—or something you're not ready for. But I'm here, Kel. I'm ready. I've been waiting six long, long months, and if I have to wait six more, or a year beyond that...I'll do whatever it takes to prove to you that I'm not the same guy I was."

Her eyes get a little cloudy, and she reaches out for me. I allow her to guide me, and she pulls my arms around her waist as her eyes find mine.

And then a question falls from her lips that I'm not expecting. "How have you changed?"

"I stopped pulling stupid shit in the locker room. Coach Bruce gave Chase and me the chance in practice a few weeks ago to show what we were made of, and I couldn't take down my friend. I fought honestly, and I won. For the first time in a long time, I *won*. And I never told you this, but I withdrew my membership at Coax."

Her brows knit together. "You did? When?"

"Last January."

"Last *January*?" she repeats.

I nod and clear my throat. "Right before Mia was born."

She looks taken aback by that admission. "Why didn't you tell me?"

"I've been quietly doing things to change for months—for myself, for Mia. For you. But you just asked me how I've changed, so I guess I'm laying it all out on the table. And to be honest, Kelly, when you went out on a date with someone else, something snapped in me. I don't want you dating some other guy. I want you to be with me."

Her eyes flick to my lips, and I don't know how much longer I can stand this close to her, her warm cinnamon scent wrapping around me and her eyes hungry for me.

But I don't dare move. I wait for her to make the first move. The last thing I want to do is scare her off, but the need echoing through me is about to scare *me* off.

"Fuck it," she murmurs, and then her lips move to mine again, and that's my ticket in.

Chapter 12
Kelly Kaplan

Six Entire Long Months

Two Weeks Until Christmas

What do I have to lose besides everything?

When he told me he thinks he's in love with me, that was everything I wanted to hear. But when he told me how he's changed, I think that was everything I *needed* to hear.

Six months? He's waited *six whole months* for me?

I've waited, too—mostly because I'm a single mom who just doesn't have time to date, but I've been holding myself back from him out of the fear that I could be next on his hit list. Or worse, Mia.

I know it would *never* be Mia. He loves her too much, and that love is pure and sweet.

But if the fear of getting hurt will always be at the forefront of my relationships since I've been hurt in the past, like Ava reminded me earlier, what am I supposed to do? Give up on love forever? Never take a risk again?

No. I think Ava was right when she said I should jump in headfirst and see where it takes me.

If she and Grayson could forgive Austin…what grudge am I holding onto?

He reaches under me, and I lift myself up and link my legs around his waist. He thrusts toward me, and I can feel it—feel him. He's hard and ready. This is far from the first time we've done this, and he knows my body. He knows my signals.

It's part of what's so addictive about him. He's ridiculously skilled when it comes to sex, and my judgment always becomes clouded when I'm around him because of it.

But this feels like far more than just sex. This feels like a renewed promise. Like the start of something big and epic and wonderful. It feels like our future is laying in front of us, and it's up to us to grab hold with both hands.

He pulls back, both of us panting from this intense kiss. "Are you sure about this?"

I nod, and he lifts me higher, tossing me over his shoulder as he carries me down the hallway. I laugh the whole way there, slapping his ass as I yell, "Put me down!"

But he just chuckles as he carries me over his shoulder like I weigh nothing at all. I guess that's just one of the fun perks of being with a professional athlete.

He doesn't carry me to my bedroom like I'm expecting, instead stopping in my family room and tossing me down onto the couch. He's hovering over me a second later, impressing me with his speed and agility, and his mouth finds mine again. We make out on the couch, and while I could kiss him forever like this, my body is aching all over to get to the main event.

I push him up off me. "I need you to fuck me, Austin. Now."

A sly smile curls his lips. "You know I love it when you beg me."

My chest races with anticipation. "Please," I whimper, and that's all it takes. His hand moves down into my pajama pants a second later, and he bypasses my panties and slides a finger right into my pussy.

I arch back as I moan at the feel of his big finger inside me again.

"Oh God," I moan, and his lips move to my neck as I continue to arch back and thrust my hips to meet his hand.

"I love seeing you like this," he murmurs against my neck. "It's hot as fuck knowing I'm about to make you come." He drives his fingers in a little harder before pulling them out to rub my clit, and I'm already seeing stars. Holy shit, he's good at this. He pulls his hand out of my pants and moves off of me, and then he pulls my shirt off. I'm not wearing a bra since I was about to go to bed when his text came through, and he stares down at me as I lay back on the couch with my tits hanging out.

I stare up at him with need, and I can't help but think how earlier tonight, I was watching my television as this man carried a football into an endzone and scored points for his team with the world watching, and now he's here, in my house, on my couch, staring down at me with lust. He wants me. He *loves* me. We share a baby.

Everything is really falling into place in a way I never could've imagined it would.

"Fuck, you're gorgeous," he mutters, and then he yanks my pajama pants down my legs along with my panties and tosses my clothes to the floor. He moves back over me, and I wrap my legs around him and dig my feet into his ass to urge him to fuck me. He's still fully clothed, but I don't care. I just want him inside me, and I can't think through the haze of lust that's surrounding me.

He thrusts his hips toward me, his mesh shorts rough against my clit, and I yell out. "Oh God, yes, do that again!"

He thrusts again, the mesh rubbing against me again, and I arch into him as he hits that magical spot.

"Are you on the pill?" he asks.

I nod, and his mouth moves to mine. He reaches between us, frees his cock from the confines of his shorts, and slides it into me.

He breaks our kiss to hiss, "Fuck," as he enters me, and I gasp at the feel of having him back inside me, back where he belongs.

Oh my God, how have we gone six entire long months without this connection?

He starts to move, and I forgot how agile he is. One of his hands is on my tit, his fingers tweaking my nipple. He's kissing me, and he's holding himself up on one arm as he drives into me over and over, pushing me closer and closer to a climax the way only he can.

"Fuck, Kel," he mutters as he pulls back from the kiss. He angles himself a little deeper.

"Oh God," I yell. "Don't stop, Austin. Don't ever stop." My voice is a needy moan, and it's like those are the key words that set him off.

"You feel so good. I can't—" He cuts himself off with a long, loud grunt, and then he picks up the speed. "I'm not gonna last much longer."

"Don't stop," I scream at him. "Faster! Harder!"

He slams into me as fast and as hard as he can, and between the way he's tweaking my nipple and the little growling noises he's making that show me just how into me he is, my body explodes into a vicious climax.

I quake beneath him, pulse after hot pulse of pleasure washing over me as I come, and he drops his lips to my neck again as he lets out a low growl before he starts to come along with me.

We lay in bliss for a few seconds after he finishes. He eventually pulls out of me, and he tucks himself back into his shorts as he gets up. He returns a few seconds later with a tissue, and I use it to clean myself up as I rise to a stand. He grabs my pajamas and hands them to me, and I put them back on as I try to come up with something witty to say next.

I'm at a loss, and I feel the awkwardness climbing up my spine. Did he really mean what he said when he got here? Insecurities plague me, but he quells them nearly immediately as he moves in toward me and pulls me into his arms.

"Hey. Get out of your head, Kaplan. That was incredible, and you are incredible, and together, *we* are incredible."

I nod into his chest as he holds me, and I draw in a deep breath of warm scent. It feels comfortable here, and I let his warmth fold around me.

He's right. Together, we're pretty damn incredible.

"Stay the night with me," I say, and he nods.

I take his hand and lead him to my bedroom, and we each take our usual sides of the bed—a habit we formed when we used to sleep together, one that falls right back into place tonight.

It feels like a lot of things are falling back into place where we left off. I just hope this time we can make it stick.

Chapter 13
Austin Graham

I Never Forget

A Week and a Half Until Christmas

I wasn't expecting to spend the night, but as light dawns in the morning, I wake feeling like everything is right in the world.

But then reality sets in.

I've never come in first before, and I'm not quite sure what to do with it.

I'm a starter now. Does that mean I'll lose my edge of competition? My entire career has been about me working to be at the top, and I found my way up here.

The only way to go is down.

I've got the girl. I lean in and press a kiss to the back of her neck. I've only had her back for one night.

What happens if she runs scared again? Or worse…if she realizes I'm not good enough for her?

I force the negative thoughts away. It's the insecurities creeping in, and I won't allow them to take root. Not after a great game yesterday followed by the night I had with Kelly.

She didn't say it back.

The thought twists its way in. I told her I'm in love with her, and she didn't say it back. She invited me into her body, so maybe that was her way of responding. Or maybe she doesn't feel the same way about me, so she couldn't say it back.

I hate that I'm waking with these thoughts today, but it's no different than any other day. I haven't been at the top long enough to banish the fear that I'll always be second-best.

But I'll fight like hell to remain right where I am.

I hear Mia's soft cries through the monitor, and I gently, softly get out of bed so I don't wake up Kelly. I turn the sound off on the monitor before I head toward Mia's room to get her.

"Dadada!" she squeals. She's standing in her crib, holding onto the railing when I walk in, and her bright, smiling face is enough to make my entire chest swell with love.

"Mimi!" I say back to her, and I lift her out of her crib and hold her in my arms. "Did you sleep good?"

She coos a little, and I don't really know what the morning routine looks like since I'm normally not a part of it, but I want to be.

"What do we do in the morning?" I ask, knowing full well that she isn't going to answer but asking anyway. And then I answer, too. "Maybe we make our own little routine while Mom sleeps."

I pick her up and start by changing her diaper and her clothes. Then I grab some books I see on the dresser, and we head over to the rocking chair in the corner of the room. I open the blinds, and I sit on the chair with my little girl on my lap, and then I start reading her the books.

We read about bunnies and rainbows, about unicorns and teddy bears, and we read a touch-and-feel book about porcupines. She giggles when I brush her finger over the textured pages, and when I glance up after I close the last page, I see Kelly standing in the doorway, reindeer pants on her legs and a sleepy look on her face.

"Aren't you two just the most adorable sight in the world?" she says, and I chuckle.

"Mama!" Mia says, and she reaches for Kelly, who gladly swoops in and steals her from my lap.

"Miamiga!" She peppers Mia with morning kisses and looks over at me. "Did you change her?"

I nod, and Kelly looks surprised.

"Thanks," she says. "What can I make you for breakfast?"

I think for a second about her surprise that I changed our daughter, and I realize...she does it all. Every day. She gets a few hours alone a week, and that's it. The rest of her time is dedicated to taking care of Mia, helping Ava, or making her wreaths. But who spends the time taking care of *her*?

Maybe it's up to me. Maybe it's something I should've been doing this entire time.

I want to show her that I'm willing to put in the time and effort to make this work with her. Last night wasn't just a one-time deal. It's a fresh start for us, and I want her to feel that this morning rather than looking back at it as some indiscretion.

"Why don't you let me take care of breakfast?" I've picked up a few skills over the years since I take care of myself. I'm self-taught through trial and many, many errors, but I can whip up a pretty mean omelet. It's a skill I put to use once or twice for Kelly when we were together before, but we didn't spend enough time together to really experiment in the kitchen the way I always wanted to.

"Since you're an amazing chef, I will take you up on that."

She sets Mia in her highchair with some Cheerios while she mixes up a bottle, and I grab everything I need to put together a decent omelet. It's simple, but it's good fuel to start our day.

While my creation cooks, I grab a bottle of ketchup from her fridge, and she makes a face at me.

"What?" I ask innocently. I already know what's coming. She's said it to me before, and somehow it makes me feel a little closer to her.

"You remind me of my dad. He always puts ketchup on everything, and it grosses me out."

I grin. "Stretch up for ketchup."

She wrinkles her nose. "I don't know what that means, but I'll take your word for it."

I make her a cup of coffee with a splash of cream and two sugars. When I set it in front of her, she looks up at me with a bit of awe in her eyes.

"You remember how I take my coffee?" she asks.

"When it's something I care about, I never forget," I say softly.

She picks up her cup and holds it in front of her mouth while I return to the stove.

I place her breakfast in front of her a few minutes later, and I scarf my own down while she takes dainty bites.

"What are your plans for the day?" I ask.

"Work. I usually head in around nine even though the place has been open for hours by then."

"Ava sounds like a good boss," I say, and I set my fork down after my plate is clear.

"The best. And the best friend."

"I, uh…you know I was sincere when I apologized to them last week. It's important to me that you know that."

She nods as she stares down at her omelet. "I know, and I appreciate that more than I can express."

I glance at Mia, who's holding onto her bottle, and I can't help but think how much things have changed for Kelly over the last year when they've stayed virtually the same for me apart from the one day a week I spend with my daughter.

It's not the first time I've realized how imbalanced things are. My career dictates my time, and Kelly and I talked about that when she was pregnant. She seems to get it, and she's never once mentioned the imbalance. Yet I still feel it, and I wish there was some way I could change that. I want to be a part of my daughter's life all the time, not just on Tuesdays.

I decide to tell her that. "I want you to know it's not just them. I want to make more of an effort with you and Mia." It's my weak way of trying to express what's on my mind even though I can't quite make the right words come out of my mouth.

"I'd like that," Kelly says. "And I know Mia would *love* that."

"It shouldn't all fall totally on you. I know it's not the first time I've said that, but if there's anything I can do to make things easier on you, just tell me."

"I know, and I appreciate that just like I did the last time you said it. But you know how I feel about asking for help, and I don't want to miss out on anything when she's little. I want to keep her close while I can." She shrugs a little and sets her fork down, her plate clean now, too. "That was delicious, by the way."

"Thanks," I murmur as an idea occurs to me. The words fall from my lips before I can stop them. "Move in with me."

Kelly stares at me, her jaw falling slightly open. She coughs a little, and then she clears her throat. "What?"

"Move in with me," I repeat, the idea taking root and forming into something I wasn't expecting.

She tilts her head a little as if she's studying me, trying to figure out what I'm getting at. "Are you serious right now?"

"Look, I'm doing what I can financially to help with Mia, but it isn't enough. I want mornings with the two of you. I want to be part of the bedtime routine every night…for *both* of you." My eyes move to hers as I make sure she catches my meaning. It's clear she does. "Like this morning—doesn't it just *feel* right? Breakfast together, you getting a little time to yourself while I read books with Mia after you did *all* the work yesterday." I shrug. "I feel like

I'm missing the small things now, and I don't want that to mean I'm going to miss the big things later."

"But moving in together…" She trails off.

"I know it's crazy. It was one night. But it's one night that's been in the making for six months and even before that, and then I went and fuc—" I glance at Mia and redirect my language, clearing my throat first. "Before I went and screwed everything up, it seemed like we were heading in the right direction." I motion between Kelly and me to indicate who I mean.

It felt like we were heading toward a future together until she decided she couldn't be with me. If last night meant to her what it feels like it meant to me, maybe we can have that future again. But we won't know if I don't ask.

She still hasn't answered my question, and I'm waiting with bated breath for the rejection I'm sure is coming. It's way out of the blue to even ask. There was no real forethought, and I don't expect her to just be ready to jump in when it's a little crazy I even asked.

"Is this really something you want?" she asks.

I can't tell by the tone of her question whether it's something *she* really wants, but I can see her thinking it over.

"I'll admit, the question just sort of came out unexpectedly when I asked it, but as I sit here thinking about the possibility…" I glance at Mia and back at Kelly. "Yes. It's what I want. It's *everything* I want."

"But do you just want it so you can be with Mia?" I sense the vulnerability in her question, and I don't know how else to make it clear that I want to be with both of them.

"I want a life together. I want the two of us to raise our daughter together and share in every moment, from the mundane to the extraordinary to everything in between."

Her eyes seem to get misty at that.

"Why don't you take some time to think about it? There's no rush, Kel."

She nods. "Okay. I'll think about it."

For now, that's good enough for me. We clean up the breakfast dishes together, and then it's time for me to say goodbye. She has to head into work, and I have workouts.

I plant a kiss on the top of Mia's head, and Kelly walks me to the front door.

I reach around her waist and haul her to me, and I lean down and press my lips to hers. I'm hesitant to let her go. It's been a fantastic ten or so hours, and I hate cutting it short.

"I don't want to leave," I admit.

A small smile tips up her lips. "You have to."

I draw in a breath that's filled with her, and I sigh. "I know."

A quiet beat passes between us, and she looks up at me like she wants to say something.

I look down at her like I want to say something, too.

But neither of us says anything at all.

"Well…bye," I finally say.

"Bye," she whispers, and then she pulls out of my arms, opens the front door, and I walk through it as I try to hold onto the feeling that everything might just work out for us.

Chapter 14
Kelly Kaplan

The Kind of Energy I'm Looking For

A Week and a Half Until Christmas

I nod as Ava adds to my task list for the day, and I jot everything down.

"Anything else?" I ask.

She shakes her head as she looks up at the ceiling in thought, and then she gasps. "Oh! I can't believe I forgot to tell you this, but all four of your wreaths sold, and I had at least ten people ask about the one behind the register. I hope it's okay, but I took down a few orders."

"How many?" I ask, my heart racing that people actually *like* the little hobby I picked up over the years.

She ducks her head a little. "Six. I hope that's okay."

"Six?" I repeat, my jaw dropping nearly to the ground.

"They already paid, so you need to get on making some more."

"I need someone to invent about four more hours per day if that's gonna happen," I say.

"Do it here," Ava suggests. "You have the space anyway."

85

I hold up the paper with the tasks she just rapid-fired to me. "After I tackle these."

"Tackle, ha-ha, get it? Because our men are football boys." She snorts, and I giggle. "Speaking of your football man, what's going on with you and the baby daddy?" She whispers the end as if Mia is listening to us in her little corner, but she's very busy bouncing like a kangaroo in her baby bouncer as she slaps at all the buttons and knobs that make different sounds.

"He came over last night," I admit.

Her eyes light up. "And?"

"And he spent the night."

"And?"

I roll my eyes. "And he banged me like a screen door in a hurricane."

"Yes!" She punches her fist into the air.

"And then this morning, he asked Mia and me to move in with him."

Her jaw drops, and she's at a loss for words. This girl is *never* at a loss for words. "Uh…what?"

I close my eyes as I nod. "Yep."

"Whoa. Are you going to?"

I lean back in my desk chair as I glance up at her. "I have no idea. The question came totally out of left field, but at the same time, I didn't say no. I mean…would it be nice not to have to pay rent? Certainly. But we've barely reconnected. I'm still working on trusting him. I'm still scared as hell."

"Of course you are, babe. And that's fine. But what if you let yourself be scared with him instead of without him?" she asks.

"I know. It's just…it's a really big step, and it felt like he was asking because he's tired of missing time with Mia."

"Did he say that?" she asks.

We both hear a loud *moo* from Mia's bouncer.

"I mean, partly. But he assured me he wants me there, too. It's not just about Mia, and I have to admit, he made me feel like he valued me this morning. He made me breakfast. He told me he wanted a more active role and didn't want me to have to do all the work." I shrug. "I don't know. It seemed like he meant it. But I feel like I need a second to think it over, you know? So we had one great night. So he apologized to you two. How do I know he's really changed and it's not just an act to get between my legs again?" I lower my voice, too, even though there's no way Mia would catch any of that over all the mooing in her corner.

"Has he ever made you feel that way?" she asks.

"Never," I admit.

"Then do it. What do you have to lose?"

Only my heart.

I sigh. Maybe she's right, but I don't want to jump into this without thinking it through.

"My lease isn't up for a while, so I have time to decide," I say.

Ava sits across from me and studies me. "Do you want this?" she asks.

I glance down at my desk as I think over her question. I think about how hot last night was, but I think about before that, when he came over after his game because he seemed to want to celebrate the victory with *me*.

Now *that* is the kind of energy I'm looking for in a long-term relationship.

It's confusing since we have a baby together, and I want to make sure I'm separating what I want as a mom from what I want as a woman.

Still, I think the answer is the same either way.

I want Austin Graham.

"Yeah, I think I do."

"Then do it. And also, get started on those wreaths."

I think through the task list she just assigned to me. It's a lot to accomplish this week on top of caring for Mia, who's already starting to fuss in the corner. And with the holidays approaching, it feels like everything just got ten times busier. So when the hell am I supposed to make these wreaths?

I'm committed, though. Ava already charged six people for them, and they don't want to wait forever.

I guess if I pull late nights, I can get it done. It's not *work* when it's a hobby that I'm getting paid to do, but I can't just invent hours out of thin air to get it all done.

I'm starting to feel like I need some help, but I don't know where to turn. Maybe it's time to take Austin up on his offer to pay for a nanny.

Jenny appears in the doorway. "Ava, we need you in the kitchen."

"Be right there," Ava says, smiling at her.

"I have to go, but I say go for it. All of it. The wreaths, Austin, the move. You only live once."

"You're right," I admit. "But with everything going on right now, I think I should wait until after the holidays to move. I think I want to do it, though."

"Atta girl," she says with a triumphant grin.

"And if you know of anyone who could help out with Mia a few hours a day so I could get moving on the wreaths, let me know."

"Are you kidding?" she asks, waving a hand in the air. "I know tons of people. We'll get you the best of the best. Promise." She knows how hesitant I've been to let anyone else care for my little one, but I have to face facts. I've had an entire year with her, and her schedule is changing as she grows.

I've never been very good at asking for help, but it's time. "You're the best, Ava. Love you forever."

"Right back at you."

She walks out of my office, and I can't help but feel like a good chat with my best friend almost **always solves my problems.**

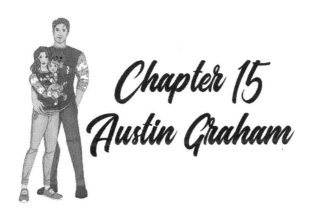

Chapter 15
Austin Graham

The Least I Can Do

A Week and a Half Until Christmas

Workouts fly by, and before I know it, I'm knocking on Kelly's door with a box of food. I texted her to let her know I was bringing dinner over. After last night and this morning, it just felt like the right thing to do. Like I'm going *home* even though I just invited her to move in with me.

My own home doesn't feel very *homey*—at least not in the way hers does. I stopped by to change for workouts this morning, and it's missing the warmth Kelly's place has. It's missing the laughter, the smiles, the smell of pine. The decorations, the lights, the tree…the wreaths.

It's missing Kelly and Mia, the two most important people in my life.

I looked around the bare walls, the sparse furniture, the half-empty rooms, and I realized that what it needs are the two of them.

It feels like everything is finally coming together for me, and now I just need an answer to the question I asked this morning.

And as I lower my hand after knocking, I draw in a deep breath as I brace myself for whatever her answer may be.

She's smiling when she answers the door, and she bypasses the box in my arms, steps onto her tiptoes, and presses a kiss to my mouth. She drops back down to flat feet as her eyes meet mine. "Hi."

I grin at her. "Hey." I nod toward the box. "Dinner's here."

"Oh, well, if dinner's here, then by all means, come on in." She gestures for me to go first, and she closes the door behind me. I head into the kitchen and set the box down, and I beeline over to Mia, who's currently lying on her back, kicking a piano that's arched in the air over her mat.

"I think I recognize 'Jingle Bells,'" I tease, and I get down on the floor to press a kiss to the top of her head.

"Dadada," she squeals, and I lift her up off the floor and pull her into my arms.

"Hi Mimi."

"I love that you call her that," Kelly says absently from the kitchen, peeking into the box to see what I brought. "Oh my God, is that Chinese from my favorite place?"

I nod, not hiding the fact that I'm proud I remembered. After all, we had one of our greatest dates ever at that Chinese place.

"This is amazing," she says, and she starts opening all the lids. "And I'm starving." She grabs some plates from a cabinet along with a variety of forks and serving spoons, and she dishes out a full plate for herself.

I set Mia in her highchair. "What's for dinner for Mimi?"

"I have a delicious vegetable chicken entrée for her this evening," she says, and she disappears into her pantry for a second before she emerges with the container. She gets a spoon and starts feeding Mia while I get my own plate of food, and I join them at the table.

She's scarfing down an egg roll, and she's fidgeting with the wrapper on the rather orange-looking delight that will be Mia's dinner tonight as Mia makes little noises in her chair that sound an awful lot like *yum-yum-yum*.

I can't imagine that vegetable chicken thing is *yum-yum*, but we'll see what the verdict is in a second.

"May I?" I ask while Kelly continues to fidget, and she looks surprised as she hands over the container. I put a little on the spoon while Kelly eats her egg roll, and I give Mia the first taste.

She doesn't grimace the way I'm expecting, and I end up feeding her the entire container.

"She was hungry, too, I think."

Kelly nods, and she stands. "I have a yogurt pouch for her, too." She grabs it from the refrigerator, and it's hard to pretend like I'm not sitting at the edge of my seat for an answer to the question I asked this morning.

I don't know how to bring it up. I don't want to push her…but I also want her to know how badly I want this.

"Oh, guess what?" she says after Mia takes the pouch between her hands and starts to suck on it.

I glance up at her. "What?"

"Ava said she took orders for six more wreaths, and there were a bunch of other inquiries."

My brows shoot up. "Wow, Kel. That's incredible. I told you they'd sell."

"I know you did, and I probably should've priced them even higher. But now I need to make six more wreaths, but I have no time to do it."

"I can help tomorrow on your day off," I say. "Unless you have something else going on."

"I need to get to the craft store to get more supplies, but yeah, that's my plan for the day."

"What if we got someone to watch Mimi so I could actually help you instead of keeping her occupied? Would you be okay with that?"

"I actually wanted to talk to you about that," she says, and she glances at Mia before she promptly bursts into tears.

"About what?" I ask gently, not really sure how to handle this situation sensitively since I'm not sure what she's upset about.

"I just feel *so* guilty, like I'm pawning her off on someone else, you know?" She wipes her tears and draws in a shuddering breath.

I set my fork down, walk around the table, and kneel on the floor. I pull her into my arms and hold her while she cries, and then I pull back and look at her. "You're not. At all. You're an amazing mom, but you're also an amazing woman. You're a teacher at heart. You're crafty, and you're talented. You're kind and positive and fun to be around. There's a Kelly in there, too, someone who is more than just a mother, someone who deserves some time to herself, whether it's to make wreaths or sit in a bathtub with a glass of wine or have her world rocked by a football star."

She giggles a little at the end, and I press my lips to hers for a second.

I pull back, and I search her eyes for a beat.

"I want to move in with you," she blurts, and my heart soars. Before I get the chance to tell her that, she adds, "After the start of the year. Things are too crazy to even think about moving now, you know? Between the wreaths and the bakery, life is just insane. Would I love to just make wreaths all day? Of course, but I have a job. And with heading to Chicago with Mia for Christmas, let's get through the holidays, and then I might have some time to breathe and focus."

"Kel, you can breathe and focus now. You don't have to work at the bakery. You know that, right?"

"Of course I do. I need a paycheck," she says, and I shake my head.

"No, you don't. I want to help however I can, and I guess I haven't made that clear. You could stay home with Mia, or you could start a wreath business and sell wreaths at every holiday, or

92

you could do none of that and stay home and watch game shows all day. I want you to be happy. You're the mother of my child. It's the least I can do."

She clings on around my neck and hugs me tightly, and it's as if I feel the stress rolling off her shoulders as I hold onto her.

I want to be here to shoulder the stress with her...not make it worse on her. And I don't think I've done a very good job of that over the last year.

But all that changes now.

For the first time in my life, I feel like I'm coming in first.

And, to be honest, I'm not quite sure what to do with that. But I can't wait to try to figure it out with the woman in my arms.

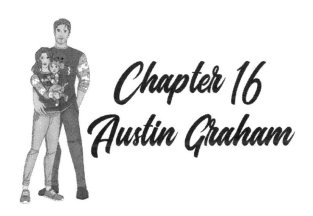

Chapter 16
Austin Graham

One of the Lucky Ones

Five Days Until Christmas

I like to take a moment at the start of warm-ups to just look around the stadium as I try to live in the moment. These moments are fleeting, after all. The average career of a professional football player spans just over three years. I've been doing this for seven.

I'm one of the lucky ones, and I know that. And to be on the field as we start our first drive when I've spent the majority of my career in the second spot feels somehow even luckier.

As I look around, I see that the stands are filling five days before the holiday. I spot Kelly, and she's wearing my jersey.

It almost feels like an early Christmas gift.

GRAHAM 41 stares back at me, and I can't stop glancing up at her in the crowd during our warmups. I'm with the other tight ends as we run through our pregame footwork drills and upper body stretches, and when I glance up into the stands, she's watching me, cheering for me, here for me. She's sipping from a huge beer, and she looks happy as she laughs with Ava.

My heart feels full. Between her and the little girl we share, it feels like my life is finally falling into place. It's everything I've worked my ass off for. And it feels for the first time like I did things the right way this time—like I earned all this. I've made things right with most of my teammates—including Asher.

We've talked a little, bonded a little over fatherhood, and have started an actual friendship.

And even though we've talked around our issues, I'm not sure I've given him the proper apology he deserves. He'd already left that day at the bakery when I apologized to Grayson, so I haven't had the chance.

We're playing the Buccaneers this weekend, and we're ready. I've studied the film, and I know the plays that I'm going to have to execute today.

Asher glances over at me as we run through our stretches. "You ready for this?"

I tilt my head a little before I nod. "Fuck yeah, I am. You?"

"Never been more ready."

"You've been dialed in all season," I say.

"Comes with fatherhood, I guess." He lifts a shoulder as his words hit home. That, in fact, is the exact same reason I'm dialed in. It's the exact same reason I'm fighting so hard on this field. I want to make plays Mia will be proud of when she looks back on game footage from her dad's playing days, and somehow making amends with Asher feels like the right thing to do.

He starts to turn away from me, but I don't let him go quite yet.

"Hey, Asher?"

He turns back toward me with eyebrows raised.

"I'm sorry I was such a dick to you and your family. None of you ever deserved that. You're the better tight end, and Lincoln was right to start you. I'm a work in progress."

He chuckles, and then he lightly slugs my arm. "Aren't we all?"

I think he might be right, and I'm learning how I need to shift my focus to gratitude rather than what I might be missing out on.

And right now, I can't think of a single damn thing I'm missing out on—well, you know, other than having Kelly keeping my bed warm every night instead of just once in a while, but that's a work in progress too—one that's about to change once we get through the holidays.

A half hour later, I run out onto the field to start the first drive of the game, allowing those feelings of gratitude to pour over me for maybe the first time in my adult life.

That's right...I'm *starting*. It wasn't just a fluke. This is the third game in a row I've started now, and it feels official.

I'm a *starting tight end* for the Vegas Aces. The woman I'm falling for is in the crowd. She's moving in with me. We share the sweetest, smartest, most beautiful baby in the world.

I have a reason to celebrate Christmas this year—for the first time in over two decades.

I knew getting that starting position would be the start to getting all the things I deserved. It's likely unrelated, but it feels symbolic anyway. Everything is falling into place. Finally.

It was a tough road to get here, but then out of nowhere, I'm here.

I'm not sure I've ever felt this...this...this *happy*.

But that's sort of the problem with flying at our highest, isn't it? There's only one way to go once you get to the top.

I just didn't expect it to all come crashing down because of one stupid mistake—a mistake that wasn't even mine to make.

We coast through the first quarter, and we're up by a touchdown as we start the second quarter. We're in the middle of a drive down the field when Coach calls, "Seam Forty-One Pepper!"

Seam forty-one is me. That means I need to run a route down the seam, and Pepper means I need to run fast and hard to break away from the defender.

This is my chance to score. This is my chance to show everyone in the stands and on the sidelines—including Kelly, including my coaches, including my teammates—what I'm made of.

It's my chance to prove I'm the player I've always wanted everyone else to see.

As soon as the ball is snapped, I sprint down the middle of the field. I'm hauling my ass toward the end zone, surprising the defense with my speed—surprising *myself* with my speed.

Adrenaline courses through me, pushing me to get to my intended target so I can catch the ball as Miles throws it to me.

I reach for the ball and grab it out of the air as I leap over the goal line.

The crowd goes wild. Fuck, *I* go wild.

My teammates slap me on the shoulder, the helmet, the ass. We celebrate for the cameras, and then we run back to the sidelines as more of my teammates high-five me. I feel like every game I get to start, I prove my worth to this team, this stadium, this city.

I'm finally exactly where I always dreamed of being, and it feels so goddamn good. I just hope this feeling can last.

Chapter 17
Kelly Kaplan

A Different Answer

Five Days Until Christmas

The entire stadium erupts into cheers as we watch everyone on the Aces celebrating with Austin.

My heart warms.

The fear that comes with watching him every time the ball is sailing through the air toward his arms and a defender is rushing toward him to stop him from catching that ball is next level.

That's my baby's daddy there on the field, and every single time, I'm terrified he's going to go down. I'm scared it'll be him lying on the ground as the medical staff and Coach Nash rush onto the field, that seconds will stretch into what feels like hours as time comes to a standstill.

What Austin and I have is complicated, and as I celebrate the touchdown with Ava, I think maybe it's time to acknowledge that my feelings for him run much, much deeper than I've allowed myself to acknowledge.

Life is short, and I've wasted the last year and a half being hard on him for something he did when he was pushed into a corner. I've wasted so much time being scared about getting hurt when I could've taken the leap and been happy with him this whole time instead of miserably alone.

I remember back to when I first met Austin and we had a few fun nights together, and I refused to be the desperate girl chasing him down.

How different would things have been if I hadn't immediately thrown up a defense mechanism where he was concerned?

He was this big pro football player with a certain sort of reputation, and I was this naïve kindergarten teacher who had no idea what she was getting into. I went into it with zero expectations, and since I'd been hurt before, I put up walls so I wouldn't be hurt again.

Putting up walls isn't really my style—or it wasn't anyway, before I had my heart broken.

Jackie, the babysitter I've used a few times now, was recommended by Ava's sister-in-law, and I just love her. She's in her early twenties and attends UNLV, and she's majoring in elementary education. It's a perfect fit, and Mia seems to adore her.

"She should be up from her nap any minute," she says as I walk her to the door.

"Thanks so much, Jackie," I say. I Venmo her the cash I promised and flash her my phone as we stand by the door.

"Thanks. Is Austin coming by?" she asks. "I'd love to congratulate him on that touchdown in the second quarter." The two of them haven't actually met yet, but she knows who Mia's daddy is.

"I'm not sure, actually," I admit. I shrug. "I'll tell him you said that." I smile warmly and walk her out, and I'm sure she was just being nice.

But Austin is hot, and I wouldn't be surprised if she was asking so she could get a little face time with the famous tight end.

You know…the guy who said he thinks he's in love with me.

I wrap my arms around myself after I close the door behind her, and I can't help the giddy little feeling that pulses through me.

I think I just might be in love with him, too.

And I think tonight might be the right time to tell him that.

My doorbell rings just as I'm cleaning up from Mia's rather messy dinner, and when I open it, I find Austin standing there. He's leaning against the door frame, and he looks freaking delicious in an Aces tee, jeans, and a backward hat.

His blue eyes fall to me, and they're heated as his gaze carries from my eyes down my body. He doesn't push off the door frame as he checks me out, and instead of feeling overly subconscious about it, he has this way of making me feel alive and sexy.

"Congratulations on a great game," I say.

His eyes flick back to mine, and a small smile pushes at the corners of his mouth. "Thanks. I credit the woman cheering her face off for me in the stands."

I laugh. "Yeah, this crazy lady a few rows in front of me kept going wild every time you took the fie—"

His mouth crashes to mine before I get a chance to finish that sentence, and when he backs up, he leans his forehead to mine. "You know I meant you. What the fuck are you doing to me, Kaplan?"

I catch his lips with mine. "The same thing you're doing to me, Graham."

He kisses me some more, and then we both hear, "Mama!"

I pull back with a small smile. "Your daughter is stuck in her highchair while I was cleaning up after dinner. Want to be the savior?"

He nods and slides past me inside, and as I close the door behind him, I can literally hear the very second Mia spots him. "Dadada!"

"Mimimi!" he says back at her, matching her enthusiasm, and my heart feels like it could burst. That feeling intensifies as I walk into the kitchen and see Austin taking Mia out of her chair. He grabs her up into his arms and kisses the top of her head, and she's giggling the whole time. I set my hand on my chest as I lean on the wall and watch the scene unfold, and this is it.

This is what I want.

I want him to ask the question he's asked me a hundred times since I ended things with him. *Are you ready to give this another chance yet?*

I've always told him *not yet.*

But today...I think I might have a different answer for him.

"Let me give Mimi her bath tonight, okay?" he asks. "You put your feet up or work on a wreath or whatever."

My brows pinch together. "Are you sure?" My tone is doubtful, though I shouldn't have any doubt that he can do this. He's given her a bath before, but always with me standing over him and offering helpful advice about how to do it.

Or maybe it's hovering. I'm an overprotective new mama of a baby girl who is used to just having me around. I can't help it.

I know I need to let him do this. I know I need to allow him the chance to prove he can, and I can't help but think about how when we move in together, I'll have someone to split these sorts of tasks with all the time. The thought of it alone is incredibly appealing, but to do it with someone I have feelings for, someone I see a future with?

How do I say no to that?

"I'm positive." He turns to take her toward the bathroom, and I stand where I am, not really sure what to do with myself.

I'm so used to our routine where I do everything and my only *free* time falls into the hours when the baby is asleep.

I wander around the kitchen for a few seconds, and I turn off all the lights before I walk over to the couch and sit. I flip to

Netflix and start up the fireplace show, and I turn on some instrumental Christmas music.

And then I stare at my tree as I listen to the crackle and pop of the fake fireplace and the soft sound of a piano playing "Silent Night."

I used to watch my mom do this very thing when I was a kid, and I always thought it was so strange to just sit and stare at a Christmas tree. But now that I'm an adult...I get it.

There's something magical about the crystal ornaments that twinkle in front of the strands of lights. It's relaxing and mesmerizing at the same time, the quiet calm after the storm of a day, and I sort of want to leave the tree up year-round just to have a quiet moment to myself every once in a while.

Maybe I will.

Austin joins me a few minutes later. He sets Mia down on her little activity mat and joins me on the couch. He sets his arm around me, and I lean into him.

If I thought it was peaceful to sit here by myself looking at the tree, it's downright majestic to sit here with my head on Austin's shoulder as we stare down at our baby.

I've been back and forth for the better part of a year and a half, but this is the moment when I know for sure that I've found what I'm looking for—that this is worth the risk.

"Ask me again," I say softly.

"Ask what?"

"The question you always ask me."

He chuckles. "Are you ready to give this another chance yet?"

I turn so I'm looking up at him. "Yes."

He angles his gaze down to me, and he leans forward and presses his lips to mine. I could get lost in him, in this moment— but there's a baby on the floor less than five feet away from the Christmas tree, and as we both hear silence coming from the activity mat that's usually a cacophony of sounds, we break apart.

Just in time to see Mia using the bottom branch of the tree to help lift herself up to a stand.

She's yanking hard on the branch, and what she's doing—along with what's about to happen to the tree—hardly even registers in my brain before Austin leaps from the couch, his skills as a tight end pushing him into quick action as he rushes toward Mia.

He lifts her to pull her away from the tree, but she's got a firm grip on that branch, and just as he pulls her out of harm's way, the tree topples to the ground with a loud crash as crystal ornaments shatter into a million different pieces all over the tile flooring.

Mia bursts into tears, loud wails filling the space that was quiet tranquility a mere ten seconds ago, and as I stare at the mess in front of me, I can't help but burst into tears, too, as I worry that it can't be a good omen that the tree came crashing down seconds after I told Austin I wanted to try again with him.

Chapter 18
Austin Graham

The Reality of My Life

Five Days Until Christmas

Oh shit.

What have I done?

One minute, we were making out. The next, the tree was crashing to the ground, and both my girls started crying.

I feel like I ruined the peaceful moment.

Deep down, I realize I'm not to blame. No one is, really. But it still feels like this wouldn't have happened if I hadn't come over tonight.

I stare at the total destruction of the tree. It's darker in here now with the tree on the floor instead of standing up tall, casting a glow over the whole room, so I take the screaming Mia and head toward the nearest lamp and switch it on.

I walk the baby over to her mother and place Mia in Kelly's arms.

"You take care of her. I'll take care of this." I gesture toward the fallen tree as she nods. I lean down and press a gentle kiss to

Kelly's cheek, and I pull back and look her in the eyes as I set my hands on her upper arms. "We'll fix this. I promise."

"'Kay," she sniffles, and she walks the long way around the couch to bounce Mia as she sings to her while I beeline for the giant mess on the floor.

I lift the tree back to a stand, and Kelly takes the still screaming Mia into her bedroom while I work. I flip on more lights and locate a broom in the laundry room, and I sweep all the little shards of broken glass along with about ten million pine needles into a dustpan, emptying it into the trash can before filling it up again. I work quickly, and I hear the sounds of screaming start to quiet as Kelly talks soothingly to Mia.

I can't help but laugh at the entire situation. I just got home from scoring a touchdown in a pro football game, and now I'm in dad mode, taking care of my girls and sweeping the floors. It's likely not what most fans imagine as they think about what the players on their favorite teams do after a win, but this is the reality of my life.

I pull the broken ornaments off the tree and toss those in the trash, too, and an idea forms in my head as I work. The tree is probably better off as firewood at this point since it likely still has some broken glass in it. A few of the front branches broke, and I think we'll take care of replacing it tomorrow. I take the good ornaments off and set them on the table, and then I haul the tree outside and set it on the side of the house. I sweep one more time just to be sure I got everything, and I make a bottle for Mia since it's inching pretty close to bedtime.

I show up in the doorway of Mia's bedroom with the bottle I just prepared, and Kelly looks grateful. Neither of them is crying anymore, and for that, I'm grateful.

"Where's the vacuum?" I ask Kelly as she walks over to the rocking chair in the corner of Mia's room.

"Front closet, but you don't have to do that."

I just roll my eyes at her since she can protest all she wants. It's happening.

I vacuum the whole area around where the tree was and around the entire room just to be sure I got all the glass, and I put the vacuum away when I'm done. I head back to Mia's room, and she's just finishing her bottle with that sleepy haze falling over her eyes.

"Thank you," Kelly mouths to me. I walk over and press my lips to Mia's head, and I listen as Kelly sings "Twinkle Twinkle Little Star." Mia's practically asleep by the time the song ends, and Kelly gently lifts to a stand and sets the baby in her crib. We both bid her sweet dreams before we head out of the room, closing the door behind us.

Once we're back on the couch in front of the Netflix fireplace with no tree twinkling beside it, I make a promise. "We'll get a new tree tomorrow. And whatever decorations you want."

"It's fine. I'm sure that's not what you want to do on your day off," she says.

I reach over and grab her hand, and I pull it up to my lips. "It's exactly what I want to do on my day off."

She leans into me and sighs, and I think it's a sigh of contentment. "I read all these blogs about parents putting up baby gates around the tree or not putting up a tree at all, but I thought it sounded ridiculous. Truthfully, I didn't think I had to worry about that until next year at the earliest."

"You want my opinion?"

She glances up at me and nods.

"I think pulling it down once will scare her off from trying it again."

She chuckles. "I bet you're right about that."

"Live and learn. I was the same way. Still am, if I'm being honest." Sometimes the lessons are good, sometimes they're a little harder. Someone can tell me a hundred times not to do something, but I won't believe it's a bad idea until I do it for myself.

But the same is true in reverse. Sometimes I'm not sure whether something is a good idea until I experience it for myself, and this whole thing with Kelly seems like it has moved to a new level where I'm ready to experience all the highs and lows of a relationship with this person.

We just had a near miss where a Christmas tree could've fallen on our daughter, but we reacted as a team. She took care of the baby. I took care of the mess. It's a simple little example that feels representative of what we could have together if we worked together instead of against each other.

"Can you remind me where we were before all the excitement?" I murmur.

"Mm," she hums, and she turns toward me. "You were kissing me because I just confirmed I'm ready to give this another chance with you."

My lips tip up, and I move them a few inches closer to hers. "Oh, that's right. Tell me what that means." I close my eyes as I wait for her answer.

"It means I'm in love with you, too, Austin."

My chest squeezes at her words. They're words I wasn't expecting, and at the same time, they're everything I needed to hear.

I close the gap between our mouths as my lips find hers, and the kiss starts out slow and tender, but the fire simmering beneath the surface quickly roars to life—as does my cock.

I take control, shifting us so she's lying back on the couch as I move over her. I slam my hips to hers, and she lets out a soft moan beneath me.

I can't wait another second without being inside her. It's almost like this entire day has been foreplay—seeing her in the crowd in my jersey, coming home to her and our daughter, hearing the words I've been waiting to hear for far too long, both that she wants to give this a try and she's in love with me.

She's in her reindeer pajama pants again, and I'm in jeans, and there are way too many clothes separating us.

I abruptly move off her and shift to a stand, and I grab her into my arms and carry her through the house and into her bedroom. I toss her onto the bed, yank her pajama pants and panties off together, and stare down at the pink pussy waiting for me. Her knees are bent and slightly parted as she waits for me to get on top of her, but I remain standing instead. I lean in between her knees and push them open wider. I slide a finger into her, and I hiss at the feel of exactly how wet she already is for me.

She closes her eyes as her head arches back, pushing her tits out, and I wish I would've had the foresight to pull her shirt off, too. Instead, I push it up while I finger her, and I yank one of her tits out over her bra. I grab her breast and lick her nipple, and she rewards me with another moan.

"Tell me how much you want it," I say, moving my finger a little faster in and out of her.

"So much, Austin. So much. Give it to me."

I pull my finger out and use the moisture to rub her clit, and her hips sway with my movements. Fucking hell, she's hot when she's all needy for me. I suck on her tit as I pick up the pace on her clit, and I slide my finger back down as I move my lips up to meet hers. She grabs onto my shoulders, her nails like claws between the fabric of my shirt and my skin, and I can tell she's getting close by the way her mouth turns a little desperate.

I want her to come while I'm inside her.

I stop everything and reach for the button of my jeans, popping it and lowering the zipper as fast as my hands will allow, and I pull my cock out. I stroke it a few times, and she sits up and reaches for me. She strokes it, too, and a little moisture leaks from the top. I wasn't expecting a blow job, but she kisses the tip and licks the bead of moisture away before she sucks my length into her mouth.

Fuuuuuck. Her mouth feels so goddamn good, and I shove my hips a little harder into her mouth as my hand moves to the back of her head. I thrust my hips toward her mouth again, and she sucks hard over me. I reach down for her pussy again, wanting to give her pleasure, wanting to feel how wet she is as she sucks my cock, but she bats my hand out of the way and lies back again.

"Fuck me, Austin. Fuck me so hard I can't walk tomorrow."

Jesus Christ.

I slide directly into her at her command, and I yank on her legs, pulling her body closer to meet my thrusts. I hold onto her thighs as I slam into her again and again and again, and her eyes are closed as she takes every hard inch of my cock as deeply as I can push it.

"Open your eyes," I demand, and they fly open and lock onto mine. I let go of one of her legs to stroke her clit some more, and I watch her eyes as she starts to fall apart. I continue driving into her, our bodies slapping together as I propel with brutal force just like she asked me to do.

That's sort of the beauty of being with someone again and again, isn't it? I know what she likes. I've learned her body, and I can deliver the pleasure she's begging me for.

"Oh yes, Austin, yes!"

Hearing her moan my name like that sends me into some other galaxy. I thrust as hard as I can, and it's too much, too soon. My body betrays me as I start to spill into her, sending her into her own orgasm, too. "Yes, yes, yes," she cries with a loud groan, and I love how this sweet, kind, sunshine woman can transform into a fucking animal when I'm inside her.

I growl a string of curses through my release, and once I'm empty and her body has stopped pulsing around mine, I drop out of her. I use her discarded panties to clean her up, and I wipe my cock on them, too, before I lay down beside her. I toss an arm across her stomach, and she holds onto that arm, cradling it close, as we both close our eyes, losing the fight against consciousness.

It's been a long day. I played in a game. I was slammed to the ground over and over, and my body is bruised and sore. I helped take care of our daughter. I cleaned up an accident. I listened to the sweetest words ever spoken by the woman I want to spend the rest of my life with, and then I proceeded to pleasure her.

And now, blissful sleep.

Maybe the *most* blissful sleep of my life.

If only the bliss could last a little longer.

Chapter 19
Kelly Kaplan

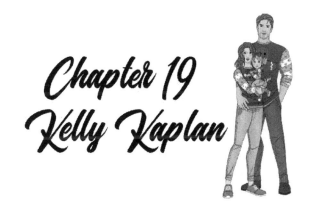

A Holiday Surprise Adventure

Four Days Until Christmas

I wake with a jolt as I hear chatter coming through the baby monitor. "Mama, Dada, Mimi, boobah doodoo boo."

Mia's awake, and she's cooing happily...for now. But like a switch she can turn on and off, it won't last forever, and the sweet coos will turn into ferocious demands like the little firecracker she already is.

I glance over and see we fell asleep right where we left off. I'm still stark naked, and he's wearing just his boxers, and somehow we slept all the way to morning after all the sex right here in the middle of my bed.

Man, he's good at what he does.

He knows my body like no other man has taken the time to get to know it, and he'll do anything I ask him to do. Harder, faster, slower, whatever—he does it, and he does it well. What a gift.

I lift his arm gently off me, and he puts it right back where it was, caging me in.

"Stay right there, woman."

I chuckle, but I really do need to get up, use the bathroom, and get dressed before Mia flips that switch. "Mia's up."

"So's Austin." He thrusts his hips against me to prove he isn't talking about the man but the dude below deck, and I moan softly.

"We should've gotten up a little earlier if you wanted to do that before we get our girl."

He chuckles, and his lips move to my neck and then down toward my tit.

I moan, not sure I can move when he's already starting with this.

"I'll be quick," he promises, and I push my tit more fully into his mouth as my way of consenting.

A second later, he's hovering over me and pushing inside me, and my head rolls back as he takes his time. He's a little slower, a little gentler than last night, but just as I asked him to fuck me so hard I wouldn't be able to walk, it's like he's making love to me now so gently that he's healing anything he might've hurt last night.

I claw at his shoulders, needing him to move faster as the ache builds inside me at the feel of him, but he doesn't pick up the pace. Instead, he slows it even more—just slow, lazy drives into me as he cranes his neck down to catch one of my nipples between his lips.

He sucks hard, driving me crazy with lust, and somehow the slow drives paired with the magic on my nipple does the trick.

"Oh God, oh God, oh God," I moan over and over as my body tightens over his, the pulsing of pleasure radiating all through me.

"Fuck, that's so hot and tight," he mutters, and he lets out a growl before he starts to come, too. His lips move back to my neck, and he sucks there as he battles through the onslaught of his release. "I love you," he whispers in my ear before he pulls out of me.

Tears spring behind my eyes at his sweet sentiment after the way he just made me feel so cherished and loved. I grab his face between my palms before he moves off me. My eyes meet his. "I love you, too."

His lips drop to mine for a sweet kiss, and then the cooing starts to turn a little angry.

She gave us just enough time, and she doesn't even know it.

I rush to the bathroom to clean myself up, and I toss on the clothes I meant to sleep in. Austin uses the bathroom while I get dressed, and then we rush together across the house before the anger turns to fury.

"Mama," she says happily when she spots me. She's standing in her crib, using the railing for balance, and she gives me that sweet little smile that melts my heart. "Dada!" she says when she sees Austin.

I can't imagine how confusing it must be for this little one to only see her daddy one day every week, but I think we're in a position to change that.

And I couldn't be more excited.

We go through the morning routine together, and he feeds Mia her breakfast while I take a nice, hot shower to ease my aching muscles. By the time I emerge dressed for the day, Austin has breakfast waiting for me—another one of his famous omelets.

"I need to head over to the Complex for workouts, but I want to take you on a holiday surprise adventure. Is that okay?" he asks.

I sit down and take a bite of omelet, and after I swallow the first bite and close my eyes like I'm in heaven, I say, "I need to stop by the bakery today for a couple hours since I'm off for a week starting tomorrow, but I can do that while you're at workouts. And a holiday surprise with you sounds really nice."

"When do you leave for Chicago?" he asks.

"Tomorrow morning." I'm nervous, though I haven't had much time to think about it. But I need to pack for Mia and myself still, and I don't have the first clue how to entertain a baby on an airplane. I don't want to shove a tablet in her face, and she's starting to get more and more active. It's not the first time we've flown together, but she was very much in the *carry me around* phase the last time, and now she's very much in the *I'm learning how to walk and don't want to be carried* phase, so I can't wait for all the looks I get from people who don't have kids this age as I do my best to parent both gently and firmly.

"I'll take you to the airport," he says.

"Don't be silly. I can just park there or get an Uber."

"It's not silly," he says firmly. "I want as many seconds as I can have with you two."

I'm tempted to invite him to come, but I know he'll just have to decline. The team has practice this week even though it's Christmas, but part of me wishes I wouldn't have booked this trip at all and I could just stay here with Austin so we could celebrate our baby's first Christmas together.

I'm excited to see my parents. They don't get enough time with Mia, and I wish they'd move out here. Maybe I can convince them while I'm in Chicago. I'm also excited to see my grandparents. They've been married fifty-seven years now, and my mom was an only child who had an only child, so I'm their only grandkid, and Mia is their only great grandbaby.

"Then I'd love that," I say. "I wish you could come."

He twists his lips. "So do I, to be honest. Or I wish you'd stay."

"I do, too. But they're all expecting us."

"I know," he says quietly. "And it's fine. I've never really celebrated Christmas much, anyway."

"How come?" I finally ask.

"I found out my parents were getting divorced the Christmas I was five."

"Oh, God. I'm so sorry," I say.

He lifts a shoulder. "It was fine. My dad basically bowed out of the picture, and my mom got remarried shortly after. My stepdad never really took to me, and I was the extra kid nobody knew what to do with. So I turned to football." He clears his throat when he catches my sympathetic eyes at him. "Anyway, that got a little deeper than I was expecting over breakfast." He chuckles a little awkwardly and shoots me a tight smile, and then he gets up and brings his plate to the sink.

But it explains a lot.

He was abandoned early on, and I don't think he's ever recovered from that.

And I don't know the rest of his history when it comes to dating, but I don't think he's been in any sort of serious relationship in his adult life until he met me. The rest were short-lived or only for one night. I think I get why now. He was scared he'd be abandoned again.

So why me? I'm the one who keeps running, who keeps telling him I'm not ready, but he continues to pursue me anyway.

It's yet one more instance where I find myself falling just a little deeper for him. There's something about our connection he trusts, and I need to be careful with what I choose to do with that.

Chapter 20
Austin Graham

Matching Sweater Day

Four Days Until Christmas

I'm surprised to find Asher in the locker room when I walk in. It's not mandatory today since it's our day off, but I've been working hard to show that I want to keep my starting position.

"You here for workouts?" I ask.

"Just finished. I usually come in after lunch on Mondays, but my son has a wellness check this afternoon, so I put in the work nice and early today." He's just finishing up, and I'm just getting started.

"How old?" I ask.

"Six months already. A whole half a year. How old is yours?"

"She'll be a year old next month."

"Tell me it gets easier," he says.

I chuckle. "I'm still pretty new at this, and I only get one day a week with her. For now, anyway."

"For now?" He bends over to tie his shoes.

"Yeah, Kelly's moving in with me and…" I trail off, not sure how to end that sentence in a way that doesn't get too deep. But then I realize that Asher and I have started to build a friendship, and if you can't talk about this shit with your friends, then who can you talk to about it?

"And?" he prompts.

I blurt it out. "And I think I'm tired of wasting time. I know what I want, and I see glimpses of it when we're together."

"Then make it official," he says. He pushes to a stand. "What do you have to lose?"

Maybe he's got a point. We've wasted so goddamn much time, and I'm at the point where I don't want to waste another second.

But we have plans today, and she's leaving tomorrow. It's not like I can lock this thing up in the next couple hours, but I'll have a little bit of time while she's gone to make things happen.

I tilt my head before I finally answer. "I think you might be right. And no. It doesn't get easier. It seems like with every new stage we stumble on, something that was hard before gets easier, but then a new challenge pops up."

"Feels like nobody tells you about those sorts of joys of parenthood, am I right?"

I chuckle as I shake my head. "No, nobody tells you."

"Well, I better be on my way before I'm late getting home, but it was nice talking to you."

He grabs his bag, and I hear the sincerity in his voice over something that should be so simple but never come easy between the two of us.

He heads out, and I head toward the weight room. Adrian is here, and he guides me through my workouts. Before I know it, I'm on my way back to Kelly's place, and I'm ready to execute some holiday fun.

She is wearing a knit sweater with a gingerbread man on the front, and Mia is wearing a matching one, both of my girls in jeans. What is it about jeans that makes babies look so adorable and grown-ass women look so bangable?

"Nobody told me it was matching sweater day," I say as I walk in and plant a kiss on Kelly's cheek first and then one on Mia's.

Kelly grins at me as she turns and walks into the house. She grabs a sweater and tosses it over to me. I hold it up for inspection, and it's the same gingerbread man.

I laugh. "You actually expect me to wear this?"

"You told me you had a holiday adventure for us today, so..." She trails off at the end, but her point is clear. Yes, indeed, she expects me to wear it.

I peel off the long sleeve tee I wore over here, and I don't miss as Kelly's heated gaze falls to my abdomen. I shoot her a wink as I pull the sweater on, and Kelly grabs her phone and takes a selfie of the three of us.

She props her phone up and sets the timer at three seconds so we can take a family photo, and I realize it's the first one of its kind.

It's not just me wearing an ugly sweater that matches hers and Mia's, but this is our first actual holiday picture together as a family. I think it might be our first family photo *period*, and that thought fills my chest with a joy I wasn't expecting.

She sets the timer to take another, and another, and another. In one of them, I lean in and press my lips to her cheek.

"Hey, send me a copy of those, would you?" I ask.

She taps a few buttons on her phone, inspecting each photo and doing some light editing before she texts four of them to me.

"Are you ready for our holiday adventure?" I ask.

She nods, and we head out to my Escalade. I strap Mia in the back, and when I fire up the engine, Kelly grins at me. "The Christmas station?" she asks, nodding toward the radio.

"Just for you."

She reaches over and squeezes my hand, and it's all because of her and our little girl that I feel a little less grinchy than usual.

I pull into the tree lot, and Kelly glances over at me.

"I figured you'd want to replace the one in your family room, and while we're here, I was thinking we could pick one out for my place, too."

She raises her brows in surprise. "Two trees? I thought you didn't really celebrate."

I reach across the front seat and wrap a hand around the back of her neck, and I pull her a little closer. "I never did. I never had a reason to celebrate. But you make me feel like I do."

I press my lips to hers as she sighs softly into me, and I can't believe how *good* this feels. How *right*.

"This is perfect," she says, and she kicks her feet with a little bit of giddiness. I feel it too—the excitement and fun of this little adventure that's sort of a date and sort of a family outing all combined into one.

We get out of the car, and I carry Mia toward the gate as my hand finds Kelly's. There's a hot chocolate stand to one side and rows and rows of evergreens in front of us. And then the magic really happens.

Little snowflakes start to fall all around us.

It's obviously some sort of machine that creates little bubbles that look like snow since we're in Vegas, and it's only going to be a high of fifty-seven today in the middle of the desert. Vegas isn't exactly known for its blizzards. I lean down and press my lips to Kelly's, and I hear Mia squeal from the side of me where I'm holding her.

An attendant with a camera around her neck approaches us. "Photo for the adorable family?" she asks.

"Absolutely," Kelly says, moving into place in front of the sign with the tree lot's name on it.

Snow falls around us as we wear our ridiculously ugly knit gingerbread man sweaters to pick out Christmas trees, and this is exactly the sort of fun family adventure I feel like I never got to have in my own childhood. It's everything I want for my own kids even though I wasn't sure I ever wanted kids. I didn't—until Kelly told me she was pregnant.

And then suddenly, just like that…I did. Mia was born, and there was this tiny little human who was part me and part Kelly and total perfection. I fell in love the second I saw her, and I'll never forget the kiss Kelly and I shared after she delivered Mia. It was wrought with emotion, and I think that might've been the moment I first realized I was in love with her.

It just took me almost an entire year to admit it to her—in part because she kept pushing me away, and I chose my moment when I finally felt the two of us starting to reconnect again.

We meander through the rows of trees as these thoughts cross my mind, and Kelly stops in front of one. She backs up and looks at it from a few different angles, and she twists it a little to look at the other side. She backs up again, and I can see the way her mind is working. It's fascinating to watch her, but she's got an eye for these things—obviously, given her talent with wreath-making.

"This one," she announces.

"Why that one?" I ask, chuckling.

"It has a halo." She says it so matter-of-factly, as if I know what she's talking about.

"A halo?"

She nods. "You know, like in those Christmas movies when they cast a light on the perfect tree with a little halo above it to show how angelic it is in its beauty. When I look at this one, I see the halo." She shrugs. "It's the perfect tree. Full, no bald spots, good height."

"And a halo," I add.

She nods and smiles. "See? You get the idea. What do you think about this one, Miamiga?"

I lift Mia closer to the tree, and she squeals and giggles.

"I think that means it's perfect," I say, and Kelly laughs.

The attendant swings by and grabs the tree to wrap it up for us as we search for one for my place next.

"Where are you putting it?" Kelly asks.

In your pussy is the first thought that comes to mind, and then I remember we're talking about Christmas trees and not my cock. I clear my throat. "In the family room where the table with the lamp is."

She nods as she squints a little, and I think she's picturing the space in her mind. "The ceilings there are, what, twelve feet?"

I nod.

"And you probably want something on the skinnier side. I saw one over here…" She trails off as she takes off for another row, and she weeds through a few trees before she pulls one out.

She spins it around, backing up to look at it from a few different angles, and she turns her gaze to me. "What do you think of this one?"

"Does it have a halo?"

She studies it a few seconds, tilting her head and backing up before she nods resolutely. "I think it's got an even brighter halo than the one I picked out for my place."

I laugh and press a kiss to Mia's cheek, and she bursts into the sweetest little baby giggles. "Then let's wrap it up."

The attendant wraps it and tosses both trees into my car as we pay. We finish our hot chocolate and enjoy the snow, and then we take off for our next destination…the craft store.

"What are we doing here?" Kelly asks.

"Well, we need to replace the ornaments that broke on your tree, and we need to buy some ornaments for my tree. Plus, I'm pretty sure someone I know has a whole bunch of wreaths to make, so we can take care of it all right here."

She turns her gaze to me, and wonder mixed with adoration is in her eyes.

I think I finally figured out how to do this the right way.

Chapter 21
Kelly Kaplan

A Perfect Day

Four Days Until Christmas

A shopping spree at my favorite store with this man who suddenly seems like he stepped right out of my dreams?

Yes please.

We strap Mia into the shopping cart and then proceed to fill the basket with ornaments and lights, bows and garland, frames to make wreaths, and evergreens to fill them in. The cart is brimming with Christmas goodies by the time we're done twirling through the aisles, and even though it's not a *date* but an *adventure*, it *feels* very much like a date, and I feel very much like kicking my feet into the air with excitement and giddiness.

This feels like exactly what I was looking for the night I met Austin. We've come a long way since then, and every moment we're together feels more and more like we're moving to the place I never thought we'd actually get to.

There's a short line at the register as we wait to check out, and Austin's phone starts to ring. He glances at the screen. "Oh, it's my publicist. I need to take this."

He answers, and I make faces at Mia while we wait.

"Oh, that's great, thank you so much," he says. "Sure, how does twenty minutes sound?"

I listen to his side of the conversation, and I feel a little jolt of sadness at his words. Of course our date has to come to an end sometime, and I need to get to packing since we leave tomorrow…but I don't want it to come to an end. I'm having the sort of lighthearted fun I've been needing, and I'm not ready for our adventure to be over.

He ends the call just as we're called up to the register, and he treats for everything in the cart—including the supplies to make wreaths.

It isn't until we're buckled into the car that smells like pine that he finally glances over at me.

He hasn't backed out of the space yet when he says, "My publicist, Ellie, has a couple of kids, and then her brother-in-law, who happens to be my team owner, had a couple of kids, and her sister-in-law had twins, and, well, she basically is running a daycare out of her house for all these nieces and nephews and some other teammates' kids. She has a lot of help, including a full-time nanny, and she said we could bring Mimi by anytime we want. I asked if we could do a trial run for a couple hours, and she told me to bring her by now. I figured we could…you know, have a little mommy and daddy time before you get to packing for your trip, and this way you could see the house and meet Ellie and the nanny to make sure you're comfortable with everything."

He wiggles his eyebrows at *mommy and daddy* time, and yeah, I just bet he wants some *daddy* time.

But I don't laugh, even though the wiggling of the eyebrows is meant to be silly and light. Instead, I feel heat pinching behind my eyes.

He reaches over and grabs my hand. "It's fine if you're not ready. I just thought I would off—"

"No, it's not that," I say, interrupting him. "It's just...you're being so sweet, and you're thinking of everything, and I think it's just going to take me a little time to get used to it. That's all."

"So you're okay with taking her over there?" he asks.

I nod. "Thank you," I say softly.

His eyes soften as they meet mine, and he offers a small smile before he leans over to kiss me. "Thank you, Kel. For all you do. You deserve so much more than I can give you, but I'm working my hardest to try."

"I know you are. I see it. I see you."

He squeezes my hand, and then he pulls out of the space, and we head toward Ellie's.

I've met her a few times, and I know she's married to former pro football player Luke Dalton. She runs her publicity business out of her home.

She's warm and friendly when she answers the door, and she leads us straight toward a family room where we find kids of all ages playing with a variety of different kids' toys. To be honest, this place seems like an absolute dream for a kid, and it's probably as good a time as any for Mia to start socializing with other kids.

A woman in her early twenties walks over toward us. "I'm Elizabeth, the nanny. Is this Mia?" She smiles warmly at the girl who's currently clinging to me, and I nod.

"Yes, and I'm Kelly. It's so nice to meet you."

"And you," she says. "Good to see you again, Austin. Mia, I heard you like *Paw Patrol*. Is that right?" She pulls a huge stuffed Skye dog from behind her back.

"Daw-daw!" Mia says proudly in her little way of saying *dog*, and I set her down on the ground as she takes Skye from Elizabeth's hands. She sits down with the pup and plays with her, and Elizabeth turns to us.

"She's in great hands if you want to take off, or you can stay a while and watch—whatever your comfort level is." She smiles, and I see all the happy kids in the room. I can see how gentle and sweet Elizabeth appears to be, and if Austin trusts Ellie and the person she hired to care for her own kids, then I trust her, too.

I lean down and press a kiss to the top of Mia's head, and Austin does the same. And then we leave.

It's weird walking away. It's not the first time I've left her with a babysitter, but it *is* the first time I've left her here at what feels like a daycare. It feels like I'll do this again—like I'll have to so I can focus on work instead of splitting my attention between two things when neither is getting all it deserves.

I hate the guilt that creeps in the second I walk away, but I know she'll be fine. She'll probably have more fun here playing with the other kids than she would at home, where I'm the main source of entertainment.

We're quiet on the ride back to my place, and as Austin pulls into the driveway, he asks, "Are you okay?"

I nod. "It's just weird without her."

"But now we can put up the tree without worrying about where she is, and then…" He trails off and moves his lips to my neck, trailing them up toward my ear. "I can fuck you on the floor under it before we go pick her up."

My breath hitches at his words, and when my voice comes out, it's an octave higher than it should be. "Then we better get to decorating."

He laughs, and I head inside to turn on the Netflix fireplace and some Christmas music as he hauls my tree out of the back of his Escalade and sets it up.

He strings lights around it while I make us more hot chocolate, and we hang the ornaments together, stopping for kisses in between, and when we're all done, we wash our hands and meet back by the tree. I grab a fluffy blanket off the couch and lay it on the floor in front of the tree, and he sits down on it first.

I straddle his lap, taking his face between my palms, and his hands come around me and settle on my ass. "Thank you for a perfect day," I say.

"It's about to get even better," he groans, thrusting his hips upward to let me know he's ready to go.

I am, too. This entire day has been filled with all these sweet details that tell me he's been watching, listening, and caring this entire time. And now we're at the moment when we have time to express our feelings for each other.

He reaches down to pull my sweater off, and I pull his off, too. He takes off my bra next, and then he pulls me close, our chests smashing together, and his mouth finds mine as his hand moves to the back of my head. His fingers tangle in my hair as his lips open to mine, and his tongue brushes mine with a fire that tells me this is going to be hot, steamy, and intense.

Just like it always is with him.

I'm addicted to this, to him, to the feelings he leaves me with, and I think that's why this has been so scary from the start. He has the power to really hurt me, but he's building the sort of trust in me to show me that he's never going to do that.

We kiss like that for a while before he shifts to pull me off of him, and then he sets me down on the blanket. He moves over me, pulling my jeans down my legs with my panties, and then he knees in between my thighs, pushing them open wide as he leans down to kiss me again. He breaks his mouth from mine and trails his lips down my neck to my collarbone, where he leaves little kisses that make me shiver. His mouth moves down to my breast, and he stops to suck my nipples. My hips arch up off the ground as the feeling of his mouth on my body sends searing signals to my pussy that I need him inside me.

But it's not time for that yet. He continues to tease me, his lips trailing down my stomach to my hip, and then he kisses the inside of my thigh, the scruff on his chin leaving a tickling burn in its wake as his mouth moves closer and closer toward my pussy. He kisses the outside of it before he slides a finger through me, stopping to focus on my clit, and I very nearly fall apart at his touch. It's a wickedly delicious sensation right where I need it, and then he lowers his mouth to my clit, moving his finger out of the way as he sucks it between his lips. I feel his tongue swirling around it as he continues to suck on it, and my God, the feeling is out of this world. I never want him to stop.

But he does, only to dip his tongue down into my pussy. He licks me there a while before he slides a finger into me, and then he sucks on my clit some more. I hear his gentle hum against my body, the vibrations sending me into another orbit, before he moves his fingers and dips his tongue inside me again. He fucks me with his mouth before he replaces his mouth with his finger again.

"Fuck, Kaplan. Your pussy is fucking addicting." He licks through me again, and he uses his mouth to deliver the sort of pleasure only he knows how to give me.

I'm about to fall apart when he stops. He pulls his cock out of his jeans and slides into me without warning, and it's everything I need.

"Fuck yes, baby, come for me," he growls, and my pussy clings onto him as he moves in and out of me. His erotic words tip me over the edge of pleasure into the abyss below, and I'm lost to everything as I writhe and thrash under him, my nails clawing his skin as I moan his name through a brutal release.

He continues to pump into me as I start to come down from the high, and he leans down so his lips are near my ear. "Watching you come is my favorite thing in the world," he says quietly, and a thrill zips up my spine at his words and the sexy, sweet sentiment behind them.

Once my body has come down from the quaking he just delivered, he pulls out of me and grabs me into his arms. He stands as if he needs no effort to pick up a woman when he's kneeling on the ground, and he carries me through the house to my bedroom.

"On your hands and knees," he demands, and I scramble to get into position. He slides into me from behind and reaches around to thumb my clit, and I feel the start of another brutal release coming for me.

He thrusts into me, grabbing onto my hips to angle himself as deeply as he can, and then he reaches around me to grab my tits. I cry out at the feel of his hands on my body as he pummels into me from behind.

"Oh fuck," he yells, and his thrusts slow and deepen as he starts to come. He drives me into another brutal release as if he's some expert in the science of what it takes to pleasure my body.

He collapses beside me, and we both hear the buzzing of his phone at the same time. He glances at his watch rather than looking at his phone, and a soft curse falls from his lips.

"Who is it?" I ask, worried that it's Ellie or Elizabeth and something happened with our little girl while we're here having sex.

"It's the team owner's secretary. There's only one reason she ever calls players, and it's not a reason I can ignore." He reaches into his pocket for his phone.

"Hello?"

I can hear the other end of the conversation through the line since he's three inches from my head.

"Austin Graham?" the voice says.

"That's me."

"This is Lily, Jack Dalton's secretary. You've been selected for a random drug test, and we need you to get to the lab within the next two hours."

He sighs heavily, but he doesn't dare defy his team owner. "I'll be there." He cuts the call and glances over at me.

"Is that normal? I ask.

"Yeah, it's standard practice, and we're all called on at least once annually. I guess this is my time, but it's not a big deal since I've never done anything that would get me into trouble. It's not worth the risk, and I realize now that none of what I did in the past was. Not when I have you and Mia in my life."

Tears heat my eyes at his words. "Oh, Austin. We are so, so proud of you. You're really turning around from where you were a year ago, and I'm finally in a spot where I can see the future and you and me and Mia, and it's so beautiful."

He leans over and presses his lips to mine. "I see it too. Are you okay picking up Mia on your own while I go do this?"

"Of course, unless you want me to come with you."

He shakes his head. "I'll be fine. Like I said, nothing to worry about."

How I wish that were as true as he convinces me to believe in that moment.

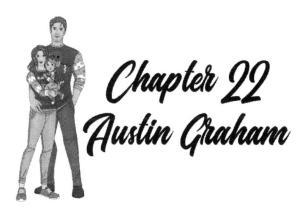

Chapter 22
Austin Graham

There's a Mistake

Three Days Until Christmas

It sucks that this is happening just a few days before Christmas, but at least I know I have no reason to be worried. I would never do anything that would risk my position, especially now that I am exactly where I've always worked so hard to be.

I head to the lab that Lily texted to me and leave my sample. I swing by my house and get the tree out of the back of my Escalade, and I set it into place in my family room. I'll decorate it tomorrow when I have nothing to do at home since my girls are gone.

And then I put in a call to my lawyer to start executing one of the plans that I have. I swing by his office to talk things through and sign some papers, and a couple hours later I'm back with my girls.

We just got Mia down, and I'm lying on Kelly's bed as she packs.

"Can I do anything to help?" I ask.

"No, I got it."

"You're quiet," I say. "Is everything okay?"

She nods. "I'm just kind of a nervous flyer. Add a baby into the mix, and every second that brings me closer to the flight gives me another little jolt of anxiety."

I stand, and I pull her into my arms. "Hey, Kaplan. You're amazing, and you've got this."

She rests her head on my chest. "I know. I'm just nervous to fly by myself with Mia. Last time we went anywhere, she slept most of the way, but I have a feeling it's going to be hard to keep her quiet, and I'll end up spending the entire flight trying to prevent her from kicking the chair in front of us so she's not bothering anybody around us."

"Hey, even if she is, anybody with kids will understand. And anybody else can go fuck themselves."

She laughs. "You know, that actually kind of made me feel better." She leans up to press a quick kiss to my lips, but I don't let it be quick.

I grab her head and hold onto her until I feel her start to give in. That little feeling of her melting into me seems to calm her. She pulls back and leans her head on my chest again.

"We never went to your place to decorate your tree," she says.

"I stopped by after I left my sample at the lab and put it up in my family room, but I haven't decorated it yet. It's fine. It'll give me something to do tomorrow."

"Aside from practice," she says.

"Aside from missing the two of you."

She offers a wry smile as she adds more sweaters to the pile of clothes in her suitcase on the floor.

"How long are you going to be gone again?" I ask.

"A week." She bends down to add some long-sleeve shirts to the pile.

"I can't believe I finally have a reason to celebrate Christmas, and those reasons aren't even going to be in the same state as me."

She tilts her head at me with a bit of sympathy in her eyes. "Then let's have our own Christmas celebration when we get back."

"I think that's a great idea."

She seems much calmer as she finishes packing in between kisses, and eventually we get naked and have more sex before we settle in for bed, neither one of us really wanting the night to end because daylight means we're going to have to be apart.

But just like every good thing, our night must come to an end.

When morning dawns, the day begins with chaos. Our usually calm baby wakes up screaming, waking the two of us as her yells come through the monitor.

Kelly leaps up. "Shit! We're late!" She takes off for Mia's room, and I glance at the clock. She wanted to get up an hour ago so we could get to the airport with plenty of time for her to get through security with the baby by herself.

I stumble blearily across the house behind Kelly, who manages to get there first as I manage to stub my toe on the couch on my walk across the house toward Mia's room.

Fuck, that shit hurts.

By the time I limp into Mia's room, I see Kelly peppering the baby with kisses as she coos *baby girl, it's okay* to her.

She's too little to tell us what's wrong, so I assume she had a bad dream. I hope it's not an omen for what's to come today since Kelly was already nervous about flying with her. I don't think waking up late to a screaming child is helping alleviate those fears.

"You go shower, and I'll get Mia dressed and start breakfast for you both," I tell Kelly.

She shoots me a grateful look, and even though the morning is more rushed than Kelly wanted it to be, we're ready to go to the airport with plenty of time to spare. It's not as much time as Kelly would have wanted, but we'll get there, and she'll still have a good hour and a half before her flight takes off.

I can feel her nervous energy as we hightail it toward the airport. With each mile bringing us closer, she seems to get more nervous. She chugs a bottle of water. She taps her fingers nervously on her thighs.

I reach over and grab her hand to try to help her calm down, and her fingers are ice cold and trembling.

"Hey, Kaplan. It's fine. You have plenty of time."

She glances over at me and nods nervously but doesn't say a word.

We are just pulling into the drop-off area when my phone starts to ring. My car's system notifies me that it's Lily. I'm sure she's calling with the test results. This will be quick, so I take the call.

"Hey Lily," I answer over the car's Bluetooth.

"Mr. Graham, good morning." Lily's voice comes loudly through the car speakers. "I'm calling with some news." Her tone sounds clipped, which is surprising for a dude who has no reason to be concerned about his test results.

"Go ahead," I prompt.

"The results are showing an anabolic steroid in your system."

"What?" I practically yell as my chest tightens. "That's not possible. Check it again."

"Your test results came back positive for Nandrolone."

"Is this some sort of joke?" I ask.

"I'm afraid not, Mr. Graham," she says. "Mr. Dalton would like to see you in his office immediately."

"I didn't do anything," I say.

"The results came back and are showing a different story. We need you here in the office."

I don't even know what to say. "There's a mistake. The lab made a mistake." My tone is coming out more desperate than I intend to, but I feel Kelly's gaze on me.

The thought that maybe she doesn't believe me kills a little part of me.

"You can take it up with Mr. Dalton. He's waiting for you."
Lily cuts the call, and my heart sinks.

Everything's been going so well, so goddamn perfect. I knew it was too good to be true.

I didn't do anything.

I pull into the spot at the airport where I have to say goodbye. I put the car in park, and she's in a rush to get out of the car. We're running late. We don't have time for this conversation.

"I didn't do this," I say. "You believe me, don't you?"

She barely even looks up at me, and I'm scared that that means it's one more reason for her not to trust me. One more strike against me to make me look like a bad guy when I'm not. At least, I'm not a bad guy *anymore*.

But when you live your life a certain way for as long as I have, of course people are going to believe the worst.

Fuck.

"We need to go," she says.

"Just…please tell me you believe in me. Tell me you trust me."

She sighs. "I know you changed over the last few months, and I want to believe you. I want to believe you've turned over a new leaf and you're not the guy you used to be anymore, but right now we don't have time to have this discussion because we have to go."

She *wants* to believe me. That doesn't mean she *does* believe me.

She gets out of the car and grabs Mia from the backseat, and as much as I want to hold her bags hostage until she gives me the answer I'm looking for, I know I need to support the fact that she is a nervous flyer right now. I know I can't get into this with her even though it kills me not to.

It should be one more signal that I've changed since I'm putting someone else first over myself and my own needs, but she's too caught up in her traveling nerves to acknowledge that.

"Well, travel safe." I grab Mia from her arms and kiss her face as my chest tightens with fear.

Close.

So goddamn close.

It was within my grasp to have more time with my little girl, more time with the woman I love. And now it feels like someone's pulling the rug out from under me.

It's as if my mistakes from the past are catching up with me, and I'm getting punished for them now. Maybe it's because I never got punished for them before. My entire life felt like a punishment in different ways. Some might even call this karma.

I pass Mia back to Kelly, and I lean down to give her a kiss. She sort of backs away, and I tell myself it's because she's rushing to leave. It's not because she doesn't believe me.

But I can tell myself that all I want. I'm not sure I believe it.

I want to tell her I love her, but she doesn't appear to be in a spot where she wants to hear those words right now.

"You got this, Kaplan."

She gives me a tight smile. "So do you."

And then she turns with her suitcase and the baby and heads into the airport, leaving me at the drop off area with my heart in my hand.

Chapter 23
Kelly Kaplan

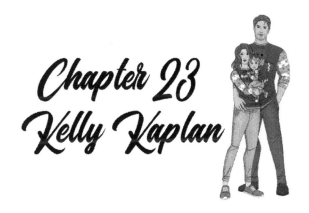

Nothing Works

Three Days Until Christmas

I tap my toe impatiently as I stand in the line to go through TSA.

I should have taken Ava's advice about the pre-check approval, but I didn't, and now I'm stuck in this long line waiting forever like everybody else.

I desperately have to pee after chugging down that bottle of water on the way here, and all I can think about is the fact that we're going to miss our flight.

And it's not just *missing* the flight but the *fear* I have of flying attacking me right now.

I have always had this issue. It's nothing new, but it still comes out of left field every time, and I really hate it.

We *finally* make it through security, and Austin was right when he said we had plenty of time. I should have believed him, but I still run for the gate to make sure the flight isn't boarding, only to discover we have an hour to kill. We go to the bathroom and alleviate at least that need.

And that brings in my next issue, which is attempting to use the bathroom with a nearly one-year-old child. This is another one of those joys of motherhood that nobody talks about. And my mom tells me it's about to get even worse once we get to the potty-training phase because apparently kids really enjoy a tour of every public restroom we should ever happen to encounter.

I'm really looking forward to that stage…in no way whatsoever.

Eventually we board the plane. We make it to the aisle seat in case I need to get out of the row to walk and bounce during the flight, but my little girl? She's an angel. I have nothing to worry about.

The little pigtails I made by gathering her sweet little locks of thin baby hair are tickling my chin as I get us buckled in, and I'm sweating from heaving this twenty-pounder through the airport along with the diaper bag packed with snacks and treats and entertainment for my little one.

An older couple boards and nods toward the window and middle seat beside me, so I get out with Mia and offer a smile. "I'll do my best to keep her quiet," I say lightly, and the older gentleman gives me a little bit of a grimace. These don't seem like kid people, and that doesn't exactly help my anxiety.

A man in a business suit takes the seat in front of us, and he doesn't make eye contact with me, but I can see the irritation on his face as he slides into his seat.

Are people really this rude, or am I just riding the high of flight anxiety? It has to just be me.

The flight is a little under four hours, and the flight attendant closes the front door and lets us know we're cleared for takeoff.

That's the moment sweet baby Mia decides she doesn't want to be on this airplane.

It's a scream that Austin can probably hear from his house miles away, and I turn her in my arms and pat her back, but she starts to kick *me* and scream even louder.

I quickly turn her back around so I don't leave this flight with a broken rib, and I do everything in my power to keep her quiet as the flight attendant starts her safety speech, but it's useless. Mia kicks her feet against the seat in front of us, and I probably should have just sprung for a seat for her where she could fall asleep beside me and her feet would've been far enough away from the seat in front of her to prevent her from kicking it. But I didn't.

The guy in front of me turns around with a glare.

"Sorry," I say, and I feel like I could cry.

And then the man next to me shushes her.

He *shushes* her!

I'm met with glares because I have a screaming, unhappy, probably scared child on my lap for the next four hours.

What the hell am I supposed to do?

I sing to her. I try to feed her, and she just throws the goldfish everywhere—including one that lands on the lap of the man beside me. I give her a toy. I play music for her. When we're able to unbuckle, I get up and walk her around.

Nothing works.

She's dead set on screaming for four hours.

It doesn't get better as we fly toward our destination…until I hear the plane's landing gear deploy. This sweet child of mine chooses that moment to fall asleep.

You know, the moment when it would probably make it easier if she was awake so we could navigate the airport and get to baggage claim. But that's not my luck today.

I'm pretty sure everyone on the plane is staring at me as we get off, but I tried to remember Austin's advice of fuck them. I quite like the sentiment, but I'm having a harder time with the execution.

I carry the sleeping Mia through the airport toward baggage claim, and that's where I spot my mom and dad waiting for me with smiles on their faces.

"Aww, did my sweet grandbaby sleep the whole flight?" my mom asks as she hugs me around the baby.

The man who was sitting beside us on the plane chooses that moment to walk by with a snort.

I roll my eyes. "Not so much."

"Well, this little angel baby is sleeping now, and she's still the most beautiful baby I've ever seen in my life." My mom takes her from my arms, and Mia continues her nap nestled in the arms of her grandmother.

I give my dad a hug, and we head over to wait for my suitcase. It's as we're on our way to my grandparents' house that I can finally take a deep breath.

Until my dad's next question. "How is Austin doing?"

He always asks about the father of his grandchild, though he doesn't know we're seeing each other again. I think, even though it's weird for him to admit since he obviously knows where babies come from, he thinks it's pretty damn cool that his granddaughter's father is a pro football star.

It's only when my dad mentions his name that I realize because of the insanity of the flight and the screaming child that pretty much drove every rational thought straight from my mind, I haven't had time to really think about Austin since we parted ways at the airport.

"He's good," I say, though I'm not really sure that's entirely true.

He seemed pretty upset over getting his results, and I really didn't have time to consider his question when he asked whether I believed him since I was running late.

"And how are the two of you, you know, with each other?" my mom asks.

"We're sort of giving things a try again."

My mom squeals. She's always told me how handsome she thinks he is—*dashing* was her exact word, but I'd just call him *hot*.

"Can I ask what changed?" she asks.

We're close enough that I can talk to her about these types of things.

"He's trying so hard to do better for Mia. And then he told me he thinks he's in love with me, and I realized that I feel the same way." I shrug, and my mom squeals again.

We arrive at my grandparents' house, which presents a whole other level of chaos as great-grandparents meet their great-grandchild for only the second time since she was born.

I sit back and take photos and push everything with Austin to the back of my mind.

It isn't until I'm putting Mia to bed that I realize I haven't talked to Austin at all today, and I'd love for him to be able to say goodnight to our girl.

As I pull out my phone, I think about how I haven't really had time to process what's going on with him. I want to believe that he's telling the truth, and yet I find myself torn.

He's going through this thing, and I'm sitting here expecting him to be at home fighting for people to believe that he didn't do what this lab is claiming. Instead, when I call him before we go to bed so Mia can say goodnight to her daddy…the call goes to voicemail.

I don't hear from him before I go to sleep, exhausted from a taxing day.

And when I wake up in the morning, I don't have a call back from him.

Instead, as I scroll through my Instagram, I see him tagged in photos from last night.

I don't really care if he goes out with his friends and his teammates, and I'm not here to stop him from doing that. But if he is as sad and worried about his reputation as he appeared to be, should he really be out drinking in public?

And the bigger question it begs is whether this is truly what I want for myself and for Mia, who's still sleeping soundly in the little travel crib my parents bought for her to sleep in here.

Do I want to be with someone who ignores my call in favor of drinking with friends? I push those thoughts away. I'm sure it's a misunderstanding. I set my phone down and walk over to the window to stare out at the gray morning. The cold, gray skies match my mood.

Snow is starting to fall, so we'll have a white Christmas. Just like the song, and just like all my memories of the holiday growing up. Mia will have those same memories.

But will Austin be a part of them?

I watch the snow fall as a deep sadness washes over me.

I would love for this to work, but I'm afraid we might be at another point where we missed our chance again.

Chapter 24
Austin Graham

A Developing Story

Two Days Until Christmas

My head throbs as morning dawns.

Going out last night was probably a dumb idea.

Scratch that *probably*.

It *was* a dumb idea, but it seemed smart at the time since I was flying solo and feeling the sting of nerves.

I had a shitty meeting with the team owner as he yelled at me for something I didn't even fucking do. I tried to convince him I was innocent, and he relented a bit—but not totally.

My track record speaks for itself, and none of my coaches believe me. They were in the meeting, too—the head coach, the offensive coordinator, and the tight end coach. They were all there, and they looked at me with disappointment.

I demanded an appeal. They demanded a retest.

I'm trying so goddamn hard not to let it get me down, but I will fight like hell for my innocence.

I just need Kelly to believe me. Everyone else can kick rocks, but if she believes in me, that's all that matters.

Asher texted me to invite me out for that beer we talked about, and I knew I couldn't sit around the house waiting for the results staring at a Christmas tree that I'm not even sure I have the heart to decorate anymore.

So I went out.

I confided in him, and I was absolutely shocked when he told me he believed me.

"If you say you didn't do it, then I believe you didn't do it," he said, and I've never felt more grateful for someone to actually believe me. It was what I needed in the moment, but I regret it this morning—or at least the drinking portion of it.

Now, I wait for test results that I shouldn't have to wait for because I know I didn't take anything I wasn't supposed to take. But then the thoughts turn dark as I start to doubt myself.

Was I drugged?

Is somebody trying to sabotage me?

Did Chase put something in my Gatorade so he'd get the starting position over me?

Hell of a fucking Christmas present.

These aren't things I should question and doubt, but because of who I am and the way I've acted towards people, they are.

That's on me. I should've treated people better, but as much as I'd like to, I can't change it. All I can do is deal with it now.

I feel shitty that I didn't answer Kelly's call last night. I was at the Gridiron with a bunch of football players, and it was loud. I'd just confessed what I was going through to Asher, and I wasn't in a place to answer the call.

I was worried I'd wake her or Mia by the time I was able to call her, and besides, the way we left things yesterday...I'm just trying to give her space. I don't want to come on too strong even though I want with everything in me for her to tell me she believes me.

Maybe I'm putting up walls. Maybe I'm avoiding her call because I don't think I can bear to hear that she doesn't believe in me.

And so instead, I'm waiting for the results of the retest. I wish I could say I'm innocent until proven guilty, but it appears I'm guilty, and now I need to prove my innocence.

The only reason I got any sleep at all last night was because I passed out, and I head to the shower to try to scrub away the hangover. It doesn't work. I walk out to the kitchen to fry up some bacon and eggs.

I walk right past the tree I haven't decorated yet. I turn on the television and flip to ESPN.

I'm only half-listening as I grab the supplies to make breakfast and start a Keurig to get some caffeine into my system. I need to beat this hangover fast so I can get to practice the second my test results come back in.

"Rumors in from Vegas this morning about the lab the Aces use for randomized testing mixing up specimens," the reporter says.

I drop an egg on the floor at those words.

"This is a developing story."

What the fuck?

I grab my phone, and I dial Jack Dalton's office.

"This is Lily for Jack Dalton," she answers.

"Lily, it's Austin Graham. I need to talk to Jack."

"I'm sorry, Mr. Graham, but he's on another call," she says. "May I take a message?"

"Have him call me as soon as possible. Please." I hang up before she can ask more questions, and I dial my coach next.

"Austin, what can I do for you?" Lincoln answers.

"I just saw a headline on ESPN that the lab fucked up some of our test results. Do you know if mine were included in that?" I blurt.

"I haven't heard anything about this, but I will look into it immediately."

"Coach?" I ask, my voice tentative regarding what I'm about to say.

"Yeah?"

"I know we didn't get off to the best start when you came in here, and I apologize for my part in that. But I want you to know I would never do something like this. I may not always do the right thing, but PEDs? That's not my style."

He's quiet, and then he says, "I know that, Graham. I never really thought you would, but you know we have to follow protocol. Human error is always possible, and I really hope that's the case here."

"I can assure you, Coach, it is. Unless someone slipped me something, I never knowingly took steroids," I say.

"I'll look into the claims you're making about this lab, and can I tell you something else Graham?" he asks, and he plows ahead without waiting for me to answer. "I like the fire in you. I like it at practice, and I like it right now. You're not backing down. Someone who had something to hide wouldn't do that. I just want to say I believe you. Maybe I didn't at first because of your track record, but I do now."

I grip the phone a little tighter in my palm. "I appreciate that, Coach. It means a lot after everything we've been through."

"Keep fighting, and we'll get to the bottom of what's really going on here, okay?"

"Thanks." I cut the call and cross my fingers as I hope for the best.

It's an hour before I hear back from Jack's office.

"Hi, Lily," I answer when I see it's her calling.

"Mr. Graham, Mr. Dalton would like to see you in his office immediately."

Everything's always *immediate* with this guy, but when you're as busy as Jack Dalton is, I guess my only option is to get my ass over to the Complex and meet with my team owner.

I show up and am immediately sent into Jack's office.

He's sitting at his desk, steepling his fingers in front of his lips as he watches me walk in and sit across from him.

"You've had some tough breaks," he says as I sit across from him.

I raise my brows and nod in agreement. "Feels like I've been fighting my whole life."

"Well, you're getting good at it. I was on the phone with the lab when your call came through earlier. I have good news and better news for you. The good news is your second test results came back, and they're clean. The better news is that your first results were skewed due to human error. The tech who collected your sample mixed yours up with another player's."

My breath hitches at that. I am in the clear, but that means one of my teammates is not. It also means that whatever teammate got called in the same day as me knows what he did and still managed to test negative.

I'm tempted to ask who it is, but I also don't want to know. Whoever it is has to have known that someone else took the fall for him when his results came back negative, and since I'm not out on the practice field today, he has to know it was me.

"I can tell you want to ask, so go ahead and ask," Jack says.

"Who?"

"Morgan."

I clench my jaw.

Jack shrugs. "I think he saw his opportunity to start and wasn't about to let it go by."

I sigh roughly, my eyes flashing with fury.

"I don't blame you for being angry," Jack says, "but think about what you would've done in his shoes before you got the starting position. Think about the things you *did* do. I think you'll agree you wouldn't have been innocent."

I know he's right, but my instinct is to protest. "But I never would have taken PEDs in the first place, and I never would've been stupid enough to get caught if I did."

He chuckles. "Just remember the position you're in now along with the reputation you're working to build when you think about how you want to handle this. Neither Lincoln nor I want to see you in here the way we did not so long ago after you and Grayson got into it."

I blow out a breath. I can't just let it go, but I also don't need this to cause irreparable damage in the locker room. He's right. I'm finally at a place that I can be proud of, and I'm not going to ruin it by fighting with a teammate—even if what he did was really shitty. I've done some shitty things myself. "Understood."

"Good. Now get your ass down to practice, and send Morgan up. I'll let you decide how you want to handle whether he gets a warning from you about what's coming up here."

I nod and turn to leave, and before I cross the threshold of the doorway, Jack says, "Graham?"

I turn back around and meet his gaze.

"Make me proud out there."

His words are heavy on my conscience as I head down toward the locker room. People rarely say those words to me. I never had parents to make proud. I was only a disappointment to my mother. I've tried to make coaches proud, and fans, and teammates, but to be second best my entire career told me I wasn't good enough.

But now, for once in my life, I have people I *want* to make proud, and I need to handle this in a way that will make them proud of me too.

I head down to the locker room and get my practice gear on, and then I head out to the field and touch base with Coach Bruce, who was expecting me.

"Welcome back, Graham."

I nod at him and head out onto the field to join in on footwork drills the other tight ends are doing right now.

I glance at Chase—who looks surprised to see me here—and I clench my hands into tight fists, digging my nails into my skin as I fight with everything inside of me to remain calm.

He has to know he's fucked the second he sees me.

"JD-Five wants to talk to you in his office," I say, dropping Jack Dalton's nickname.

His eyes widen a little as if he knows he's caught.

"I know what happened," I say to him, and I draw in a deep breath as I get up in his face. He flinches a little. "I understand why you did what you thought you had to do. I will not forget, but I think you are going to pay the price without me being the one who's issuing the punishment."

He nods once at me as if he understands what I'm saying. He turns to talk to Coach Bruce for a second before he excuses himself to head upstairs.

I have a feeling my name will be in the news over the next couple days, and that's okay. Two days from now is Christmas, and the coaching staff decided to have us practice today and tomorrow and give us Thursday off to spend the day with our families since our game this week is a home game.

But as I'm practicing on the field, I realize what I want.

What I *really* want.

What I've always wanted.

What's been within my grasp all along.

I need to go get it, to hang on tight to it, and to never let it go.

I'm not spending Christmas at home by myself.

As soon as I get home from practice, I'm booking a ticket to Chicago.

Chapter 25
Kelly Kaplan

A Conversation I Need to Have in Person

Two Days Until Christmas

"We haven't seen snow like this in years," my grandma says as she whips up the batter for her famous pancakes so we can eat breakfast for lunch—her favorite meal to make. "Good thing you got in yesterday, or your flight might've been canceled."

I murmur some sound to let her know I'm listening, but I'm not all that focused on our conversation. I can't stop brooding over the fact that I called him last night and he never answered.

I know he has practice today, so I know he's awake by now...but he still hasn't bothered to call. All the progress we made feels like it's being pulled out from under us, and he is reverting back to this guy that I'm not sure I can trust.

I glance over at Mia, who's sitting on my dad's lap as they watch *Sesame Street*, and can't help but think she deserves everything. I thought we were in a position to give that to her, but I'm not so sure anymore.

My mom walks over and slings an arm around my shoulder. "Did you two sleep good last night?"

I nod. "Mia was worn out from all the screaming, and so was I." I chuckle. "You?"

"Just fine," she says. "But if you slept good, why are you so cranky today?"

My brows pinch together. "I'm not cranky." I definitely sound cranky, and she raises her brows pointedly.

"Your grandmother is making her famous pancakes, and you're sitting here at the table, staring out the window instead of standing at her feet to help like you did when you were little."

"I'm not little anymore," I protest.

"No, that's definitely true, but I don't know...I guess I just figured you would pass the torch to a little one, and instead you're sitting here like you just lost your best friend."

"I'm fine." I should've known that I couldn't hide all this from her, so I relent and give her the truth. "I called Austin last night and he didn't pick up, okay? And then I saw pictures of him out with friends. It just sucks, and I have no idea what's going on."

"So call him again," she says.

"He's got practice today, and he didn't call me before he left. He's going through some things, and I'm trying to be understanding and give him space, but seeing pictures of him out with his friends when he can't be bothered to call his daughter to say goodnight, let alone the woman he is supposedly trying to rekindle things with...it just hurts." I brush away a tear I didn't even realize fell.

My grandma walks over and puts an arm around my shoulder. "Sweet, sweet Kelly. Trust me when I say men don't think the way we do. I'm certain you're reading too much into this, and things will look different once you are able to talk to him in person."

I know she's right, and I'm trying to be understanding, but I can't help thinking that even though I know the game will always have to come first to him...I still wish he would put us first. I don't say that to my mom and grandma, instead just opting to smile like they're right.

And maybe they are. But they also don't know all the details about our complicated history.

I know he's going through this whole thing with the drug test, and as I laid in bed last night, thinking about him and his reaction to the results, I realized that I believed in him wholeheartedly. There must be some mistake with the results.

But because he didn't pick up his phone and I wasn't able to tell him that, who knows where his mind is now? Is he thinking I don't believe him?

It was a whirlwind, and I didn't have time to think things through. It wasn't until the quiet of night, when Mia was asleep and the house was silent, that I realized I don't have any doubts about him at all.

But I can't fix that when I'm hundreds of miles away.

Lunch is ready, and the pancakes are as delicious as I remember. We even give Mia a little one, and she gobbles it up. I guess we have another new food to add to her dietary variety even though I don't make pancakes anywhere near as delicious as my grandma's.

I take Mia outside for a while as the snow falls relentlessly. It's peaceful and quiet here, and it's a beautiful thing to watch my sweet little girl experience her first blizzard.

I take videos, thinking about how I can send them to Austin when it strikes me how *every* thought seems to revert back to him somehow.

This isn't how I pictured feeling on Christmas, and I have the sudden urge to get back home to him.

I want to spend the day with him even though I know he'll be at practice for a portion of it. We're trying to build something here, and I've spent enough time brooding over him not calling me last night.

I want him to know that I believe in him and trust him, and that I don't care what the test results said. If he says he didn't do it, then I believe he didn't do it, and that feels like a conversation I need to have with him in person.

I want him to know that he comes first to Mia and me. I feel like that is something he *needs* to know, but I had this trip planned, and so I took off to Chicago without a second glance back when we should be spending Mia's first Christmas together as a family.

I head back inside and run upstairs to change Mia out of the cold, wet clothes from playing in the snow. I grab my phone and check to see when the next flight back to Vegas is, but trying to get a flight out on the night before Christmas Eve last minute is next to impossible.

The only one with a seat available is the redeye tonight.

I don't think it's right to put Mia through that. Maybe she'll sleep the whole time, but I doubt it. I head back downstairs and plop down onto the couch next to my dad. I set Mia on his lap, and he glances over at me.

"You okay?" he asks.

I press my lips together, and then I go for the truth. "I feel like Mia and I should get back home to be with Austin on Christmas, but all the flights today are booked except the redeye. I don't think I should take Mia across the country two days before Christmas on a redeye flight after the way she behaved on the flight out here."

He chuckles. "Why do you feel like you should go back home?"

"Real talk?" I ask.

"Always."

"He was drug tested a couple days ago. The results came back positive for a performance-enhancing drug. He said he didn't do it, that there had to be a mistake. We were in the car on the way to the airport, and I didn't really have a chance to tell him I believe him. It was chaos. We were late for our flight, but I called him last night, and he didn't answer because he was out drinking with his teammates. And now I don't know where we stand or if he thinks I don't trust him, and I hate that."

My dad leans his head against mine. "Want to know what I think?"

"I would love to know what you think."

"I think if you belong together, you'll find a way to make it work. And he was out with his friends. He's going through something, his girl and his daughter are out of town, and maybe he just needed a night to blow off some steam with his friends. Guys do that, Kelly Belly. It's not like he was out with some other woman. Have you tried calling him again?"

I shake my head. "He's at practice now."

"Two days before Christmas?"

I nod. "They play Sunday, so it's a regular week for them."

"Is that hard on you?" He bounces Mia, and she giggles.

"It's hard being away from him for Christmas, but I kind of know what I'm getting into in terms of his schedule."

"I just want you to be happy, and I know it's been a tough road for you to get there with him. But if you're willing to put in the work, I think you could have exactly what you're looking for."

"But what does *put in the work* even mean?" I ask. "Does it mean traveling across the country two days before Christmas to get to him so I can tell him I believe him?"

"It might," he says with a shrug. "But there's a kid to think about here too, so maybe it means being patient and trusting that he's on the other end of us waiting for you. But I don't think it means that you should sit around here with that sad look on your face anymore. You're here to celebrate Christmas, so enjoy it while you're here, and then you get back home to him and work it all out."

I lean on his shoulder. "You're pretty good at this advice thing."

He chuckles. "I aim to please." Mia starts rubbing her eyes, so I take her upstairs to get her down for a nap. The adults play a rousing game of Uno with my grandfather emerging victorious.

I check my phone but still don't have anything from Austin, and I try to remember my dad's words about being patient.

Maybe he's right. I've spent far too much time since I met him not trusting him and believing the worst, which has amounted to a rather colossal waste of time.

And since I still don't have a call or text from him, I realize it's okay for me to try again. I don't have to wait forever for him to call.

Me: *Hope practice went well today. Thinking about you, missing you, and thought I should tell you that of course I believe you.*

And then I wait.

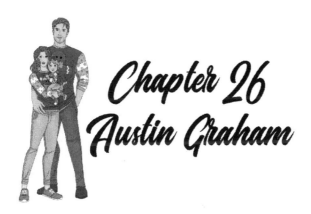

Chapter 26
Austin Graham

Delayed

Two Days Until Christmas

I stare at the message as I try to come up with the right response. I don't really have the words that could properly express how it means everything to me that she believes me.

And that's why I feel like I want to wait until I'm in person to properly thank her for that.

I'm also afraid if I call her and talk to her that I will blow the surprise. I'll do something stupid like end the conversation with *see you soon* or something equally dumb that would give away the fact that I have a ticket on a flight tomorrow after practice. It'll get in late, and I'm not even sure exactly where her grandparents live, but I figure I'll make up a story about wanting to send a gift so I can get their address ahead of time.

I decide to text back rather than call even though I want nothing more than to hear her voice and Mia's. I glance at the clock and realize Mia's sleeping by now anyway. I also realize that she doesn't know that if I was in trouble because of the drug test, I wouldn't be at practice.

Me: *That means everything to me. I miss you both and I'm sorry I've been quiet. It's been a brutal week.*

I leave it at that even though it's vague, and I head to bed. I'm up and at 'em early in the morning for practice, and I see a reply from her.

Kelly: *Sorry it's been brutal. Wish I was there to help.*

She *is* helping, and she doesn't even know. She has no idea how just that one little text telling me she believes me was exactly everything I needed.

I have the trust and faith of somebody who means everything to me.

I head to practice, and I'm a little early.

Asher is in the locker room, the only one here as early as me. "Merry Christmas Eve," he says.

I nod. "Same to you." I sit on the bench inside my locker and start changing shoes.

"What are your plans for the holiday?" he asks.

"Kelly is in Chicago with her family, so I decided to grab a flight out tonight after practice to spend Christmas with them."

"Wow. You're really all in on that, huh?" he says.

"Yep. A hundred percent." I finish tying my left shoe and get started on the right.

"You are a different guy with her and your daughter."

"It means a lot that you noticed. I've been working hard to make them proud of me in part because I've seen that it can be done through people like you." He knows I'm referring to when he first got here and ended up suspended for an entire year.

That was my year. My chance to prove who I was as a player, and I did well. But the second his suspension was over, he was back on the field in the place where I was supposed to be. Is it any wonder why I had a grudge against him?

It took having a kid and looking at who I was becoming as a man to help me check my ego. It's because of Mia that I can admit that Asher Nash is a better tight end than I am, but that doesn't mean I can't keep trying anyway.

He walks over and slaps me on the shoulder. "You know, Graham," he says. "I wish this was the guy who greeted me when I first came to the team. We could've been working together this whole time instead of against each other. We could've been good friends from the start."

"You're right. And I'm sorry for that, but it's never too late, right?"

He nods. "You hear about Morgan?"

I shake my head. "How long?"

He shrugs. "I don't know, but I imagine it'll be whatever the league hands down plus some extra from the Aces."

"Yeah, stupid move on his part. Do you think it's the end for him?" I ask.

He shrugs. "No idea, but one thing I do know is that there's always time for second chances."

This guy is really a great player, and the more I give him a chance, the more I see he's a pretty good dude too.

Coach works us extra hard in practice since we have a random midweek day off to recover. Once practice is over, I head home and grab my bag to get to the airport. I check in for my flight and see it's delayed.

I blow out a breath. This isn't getting off to a good start, but I'm determined, and a determined Austin is one that will stop at nothing to get what he wants.

I was already getting in after ten in Chicago, and now it looks like I won't be getting in until after midnight, so it kind of seems like my options are limited if I'm going to surprise her since she'll be sleeping.

I shoot her a text.

Me: *I would like to send something to your grandparents' place. Can you send me their address?*

She replies with the address so I know where I'm going once I land.

I try to hold onto some semblance of patience as I wait at the airport for my delayed flight. I play games on my phone. I grab a bite to eat. It's Christmas Eve, and all I want to do is be with my daughter and the woman I plan to spend the rest of my life with.

Instead, I'm stuck in an airport in Vegas waiting for a flight that is now showing that it's delayed another hour.

I've been waiting for two days for this moment to arrive—to get on a plane and head toward my girls to surprise them with this huge gesture and give Kelly the gift I've been preparing the last few days. It feels like nothing is nearly as important as getting on the plane and getting to Chicago.

That's when I hear an announcement.

"Flight 3741 with service to Chicago O'Hare is now taking off at eleven thirty-six."

Fuck.

It's another delay.

I head up to the counter, feeling a whole lot like the mom in that movie where they leave the kid at home and she's at the airport begging for a flight to Chicago.

"I know it's Christmas Eve, and I'm sure you just want to get home and be with your own family, but do you know of any way I can get out to Chicago tonight?" I'm begging, and I lay it on extra thick. "I have tomorrow off, and I'd love to be able to spend Christmas with my baby. It's her first. Do you have kids?"

She nods. "Two. I'm so sorry, but the flights going into O'Hare are grounded because of the blizzard hitting the city right now. There's nothing I can do." She presses her lips together apologetically.

"Is this flight going to be canceled?" I brace myself for the inevitable truth.

"More than likely, yes." She leans in closer to me. "I'm a huge fan. Because of that I'm going to tell you a secret. Our airline doesn't fly into Midway, but there are flights going out tonight, and one is taking off from gate B12 in twenty minutes. If you rush over there and they have room, which they do since I just called over to ask, they might be able to get you out tonight."

Her words feel like a Christmas miracle, and I lean over the counter to give her a hug. She laughs, and I pull my phone out and open my contacts. "Put your name and number in here, and I'll set you up with four tickets to Sunday's game."

Her jaw drops as she types in her details. "My husband is going to die when I tell him this."

"Well, for both of your sakes, I hope that's not true, but we'll see you on Sunday."

"Thank you," she says.

I shake my head. "Thank you." I emphasize the *you* and run over to B-twelve.

Chapter 27
Kelly Kaplan

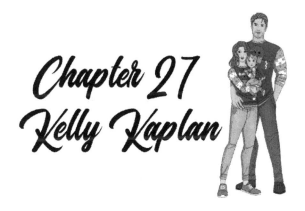

Canceled

Christmas Eve

I stare at the word flashing on the board beside my flight
number.

Canceled.

It flashes again and again as if to mock me. Canceled.
Canceled. Canceled. Canceled.

I walk over toward the window where my plane should be
parking any minute and instead watch the snow as it falls like a
blanket over the city.

I decided to book the redeye. I figured I'd deal with Mia. This
is too important to miss, and so I need to get to him for
Christmas.

Mia is asleep in a little umbrella stroller, so at least she doesn't
have to listen to me sniffling the way she would if I was holding
her in my arms as I call my mom.

"My flight was canceled," I wail when she answers.

"Oh, honey, I'm so sorry. This storm is wicked, so it's probably
for the best. We'll get you out in a couple days once it clears up."

The hope for a desert Christmas is squashed by the actual white Christmas I apparently was meant to have.

"Dad is about a half hour away from you, so I'll call him and let him know to turn around and get to you. Give him a little bit of time to get to you, okay?"

"Thanks," I mutter, and then I try to figure out what the hell I'm going to do for the next half hour.

I slide onto one of the chairs and watch some planes move down the runway. Some flights are still going out tonight, and I don't understand why the chosen few can come and go, but I can't get out tonight.

A plane lands and pulls into the gate that was supposed to be the one I took off from. That should be my plane, the one carrying Mia and me toward Austin so we could celebrate our first family Christmas together.

I stare at that damn plane and watch it park. The door opens, and the first passengers start to disembark.

I'm not really sure what to do with myself. I don't really want to wait for my dad to come pick me up sitting at this gate for my canceled flight, and I need to go track down my suitcase anyway. With that in mind, I stand. I'll find my suitcase and then wait near the arrivals pickup area since I know that's where my dad will be.

I sling the diaper bag on my shoulder and grab the handles of the stroller. I turn away from the gate to start walking in that direction, and that's when I hear it.

"Kelly?"

I freeze at the sound of my name, and then I whip around…and I see Austin Graham standing there.

He's wearing a baseball cap pulled down low over his eyes and the gingerbread man sweater paired with jeans…and I'm pretty sure I'm hallucinating because there's no way Austin Graham is standing in front of me in the airport calling my name.

We stare at each other across a span of about ten feet, both of us frozen for a few beats except for my heart, which is beating practically out of my chest.

And then he strides toward me, closing the gap between us.

I feel his arms as they come around me, telling me this is real—I'm not hallucinating.

He's really here. He's really, actually here.

He came for me.

I wrap one of my arms around his neck, the other protectively still on the stroller handle, and I stare up into his eyes.

At the exact same time, we both ask, "What are you doing here?" And then we both start to laugh.

"I booked a flight because I had to see you, but it was canceled," I say at the same time he says, "I had to get here to spend Christmas with my girls."

I cling to his neck as his lips crash down to mine, and we kiss right there at the gate at the airport, both of us feeling the beautiful wonder of being together again.

I pull back. "I had to tell you in person that I believe you, Austin. Whatever happens, if you say you didn't do it, I don't doubt that for a second. I want you to know that you come first for Mia and me, and I never should've gone to Chicago without you when all I want is to spend her first Christmas together as a family."

"That's why I'm here," he says, and he leans down to kiss me again in between sentences. "I had to be with you. Coach had us practice yesterday, and we have tomorrow off, and even if we didn't, I would've skipped practice and paid the fine to get here to you."

My jaw slackens at that. "You would've paid the fine?"

He nods. "Oh, and one more thing. I was cleared." His lips tip up.

"What?" I breathe.

"I was cleared. Turns out my sample was switched with someone else's. I retested, and then the lab admitted the mistake. My retest came back negative. But I have to tell you, Kaplan, it means everything to me that you believed in me before you knew. I wanted to call you and tell you, but I just knew if I did, I'd blow the surprise that I was planning to come here."

"*That's* why you haven't called me?" I ask stupidly.

He laughs. "The first night when you called, I was at a bar, and it was too loud to answer. I thought about calling you back once I was home, but I didn't want to wake you." He kisses me again. "Thank you, Kelly," he says, his voice low and raspy.

"For what?"

"For believing me. For believing *in* me. For waiting for me."

Tears pinch behind my eyes. "Thank you, Austin."

"For what?"

"For showing me how we come first to you."

We share another kiss that starts to turn heated, and I pull back when my phone starts to ring. It's my dad.

I pick up. "Dad?"

"I'm about ten minutes away," he says.

"Okay, I still need to grab my suitcase. I'll text you once I have it."

"Sounds good. Sorry about the cancellation."

"Thanks, Dad. I'll see you soon." I end the call before I ruin the surprise, and we turn to head toward baggage claim with Austin pushing the stroller.

I keep glancing over at him in a bit of shock.

He's here. He's really here.

It feels like it's shaping up to be the merriest Christmas I've ever had.

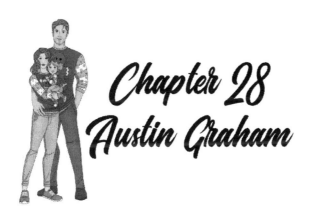

Chapter 28
Austin Graham

Down in the Basement Where Nobody Can Hear Us

Christmas Eve

When we both have our suitcases, she texts her dad to let him know she's on her way out. I gently take Mia out of the stroller since she's sleeping, and I press a kiss to her cheek before I hand her to Kelly. I close up the stroller and set it on top of my suitcase, and I roll my suitcase and Kelly's out to the curb where her dad is waiting for us.

He looks downright shocked when he gets out of the car to help with her suitcase and he spots me.

We've met a couple times since her parents have been out to visit her and Mia, and he's always struck me as a great guy who doesn't seem to hate me.

"Austin, what are you doing here?" he asks, and he gives me a hug.

"I just ran into your daughter here at the airport," I say with a shrug, and he laughs.

"Why do I feel like there's more to that story?" he asks.

"There is, but we'll tell you in the car," Kelly says through chattering teeth. She straps Mia back into the car, and she slides into the backseat to give me the front as we load the suitcases into the trunk.

The heat is blasting out at us as we navigate toward her grandparents' house, and we finally fill her dad in on what happened.

"She was hanging out at the gate after her flight was canceled," I say. "Mine landed, and I spotted her there in the terminal, and somehow, even though my flight was delayed and I wasn't even sure I'd make it here, we ran into each other."

It sounds an awful lot like fate stepping in, as if we were meant to be able to spend Christmas together, and I'm so glad we didn't miss each other.

We pull up to her grandparents' house shortly after that, and Mia is still sleeping soundly—as are Kelly's grandma and grandpa. Her mom is still awake, however, and she looks shocked to see me standing behind Kelly lugging two suitcases into the house.

"Austin?" she asks, and she stares at me as if she's hallucinating—much like her daughter did when she first saw me.

"Hey, Mrs. K," I say, and I abandon the suitcases in the entry to walk over and give her mom a hug.

"This is sure a surprise," she says. "What are you doing here?"

We recount the story of the airport to her, too, and she just smiles warmly.

She squeezes my shoulder as she shakes her head. "Of course that's how it happened. You two are just meant for each other, and I'm so happy it worked out so that you can spend the holiday with us."

We chat a little longer in the entry, and when her parents seem like they're ready to head up to bed, I ask, "Where can I find wrapping paper and supplies? I couldn't bring wrapped presents on the plane, and I have a few things."

Kelly glances over at me. "You didn't have to do that."

"They're not for you," I tease, and she giggles as she holds up both hands.

"All the stuff is down in the basement," she says. "Let me get Mia up to her crib, and I'll take you down and help."

I raise a suggestive brow at her that only she catches, and she definitely gets my meaning.

We won't be alone up in the room we're sharing with Mia—if I'm even sleeping in that room. I don't know the rules here in this house, though I assume that's where I'll be tonight. Regardless, the room is out with our daughter sleeping next to us.

But maybe down in the basement where nobody can hear us...

Okay, fine. *Definitely* down in the basement where nobody can hear us.

We head downstairs. The main section is furnished with a couch, a coffee table, and a television in a huge entertainment center, and a wall sections off an unfinished storage area. Against the far wall is a bar complete with a countertop and stools, and that's where I spot the supplies for wrapping gifts.

"I may or may not have been down here earlier using all this stuff, and Grandma told me to just leave it on the counter," Kelly says. We walk over, and she shows me the supplies. She perches on one of the barstools, and I set the duffel bag packed with gifts onto the counter.

I move in between her legs and angle my head down so our eyes connect, and a heated moment passes between us. I wrap a hand around her neck and pull her in close as I drop my lips down to hers.

She pulls back a little, her eyes moving to mine. She draws in a deep breath and lets it go, and it's as if she's been holding onto that for some time. Her shoulders seem to relax as she says, "I can't believe you're really here."

I lean my forehead to hers. "Do you need me to prove it?"

"If that means what I think it means, then yes."

I shove my bag and the wrapping supplies out of the way and lift her off the stool to prop her onto the counter. A gasp escapes her at my sudden movement, and I move between her legs, one hand moving immediately up her shirt as my hand settles on her tit. My mouth moves to hers. She arches her back to push her tit into my hand, and her mouth is urgent on mine.

How did we go so goddamn long without this?

I reach between us to feel her pussy over the jeans she's wearing, and I have to get her out of those. I need to taste her like I need to breathe.

I flick the button, and she holds on around my neck to lift her ass off the counter as I pull them down her legs along with her panties, stripping her bottom half bare. I shove her knees apart, bend down, and slide my tongue through her slit.

She's so wet for me, and she tastes like pure heaven.

She moans as I tease her clit, circling my tongue around without sucking on it, and her hands find the back of my head. She holds me in place, encouraging me to continue what I'm doing as I lick my way through her slick folds.

She arches her back, and when I dip my tongue inside her, she starts to tremble.

She's too high up on the counter for me to kneel, and I can't keep this angle going for long, but fuck...I never want to stop tasting her. I hum against her pussy, and she widens her legs further as she starts to thrust.

God, I love her. She's desperate for release, and she grinds her pussy against my face. I meet her thrusts, sucking and licking as she moans for more, and I pull back to slide my finger into her. I move to a stand, and I kiss her, swirling my tongue against hers. I shove two fingers into her and use my thumb to tease her clit as I pull back just enough to say, "Taste yourself on my tongue."

I swirl my tongue against hers some more as I continue to finger her, and I can tell by the way she starts to claw desperately at my shoulders that she's moments from falling apart.

I need to be inside her when she comes. I need to feel the way her pussy tightens over my cock as she takes every inch of me inside.

I pull my fingers out of her and lift her back onto the barstool to give me the right angle as she protests, and I yank my cock roughly from the confines of my jeans. I stroke it a few times, and she pulls off her shirt and bra, exposing those gorgeous tits for me as she sits naked on a barstool in this basement.

Jesus, she looks hot sitting there like that. I bend down to suck her nipple between my lips, and she groans as she reaches for the cock I'm still stroking. She bats my hand out of the way and uses both her hands to move up and down my shaft, and fuck, it feels good. Too good. So goddamn good that I'm going to come way too fast.

She hops off the stool, gets down onto her knees, and sucks my dick into her mouth. I reach down with both hands to tweak her nipples while she works me with her mouth, and the feel of her tits in my hands and her mouth on my cock is sheer perfection.

She swirls her tongue around the tip before she takes my length all the way to the back of her throat. She moans around my cock, like sucking on me is getting her off, too, and the vibration of her hum nearly sends me into my orgasm. She sucks as she moves her hands along my shaft, bringing me closer and closer to the edge. I let go of her tits to hold onto the back of her head, and I thrust my hips so I bump the back of her throat on her way back down.

She moans again.

"You like that?" I mutter through the pleasure, my voice raspy and gritty as I clench my jaw and try to hold on for longer.

"Mm," she murmurs around me, and then she pulls me out of her mouth and slides her tongue down my length toward my balls. She sucks them gently into her mouth one at a time, and fuck, that familiar fire rips along my spine, the signal that I'm not far.

She handles my cock in a way nobody else ever has, and I think it's because she handles *me* in a way nobody else ever has. She's gentle and loving, but she also knows how to put me in my place, and she knows how to fuck like an animal.

She's everything I've ever wanted in a woman.

She licks up my shaft again, and then she moves to a stand.

"You're not done," I say, motioning to my rock-hard cock that's begging for release.

"Neither are you." She pushes my jeans all the way down, and I kick them off. She yanks my sweater off so we're both naked, and then she pushes me onto the stool. She climbs on top of me and slowly slides her pussy down onto my cock, and she spins the seat of the stool so she can grip onto the countertop behind me for balance.

She bounces up and down my cock, and I grip onto her ass as I let her control our pace. Her tits are right in front of my face as she arches her back toward me, and I suck one of her nipples into my mouth. I continue holding onto her ass with one hand, but I let the other inch over closer to her entrance. I press a finger to the tight ring, and she seems to lose all control as I feel the tightness of her ass along my finger. I'm sucking her nipple, she's slamming down onto my cock, and I'm fingering her ass all at once, and it's too many sensations.

I feel her body starting to tighten over me as her grinding becomes wild, and it's enough to drive me to climax.

"Oh God, Aust—Austin!" she cries, and she buries her head into my shoulder, her nails digging into the flesh of my back as I continue moving my finger in and out of her ass in rhythm with the pace she's setting.

"Yes, baby, come all over my cock," I grit out, and my body lets go as she continues to slam down onto me. "Oh, fuck! I'm coming," I grunt, and I erupt into her, filling her as our bodies continue to move together with this white-hot pleasure.

We're both panting as we come down from the high of that climax, and she's resting her head on my shoulder, her face turned into my neck as I ease my finger out of her ass. She leans forward to press a soft kiss to my neck, and I pull back a little so I can catch her lips with mine.

We kiss softly for a few beats in the quiet afterglow, our bodies sweaty but still connected, and eventually she lifts off of me.

"I thought you were going to pinch me to prove you were really here, not give me the hottest climax of my life," she says as she gathers her clothes.

I laugh, and I'm not quite ready to move yet, but I know I need to. I force myself off the stool, and I give her ass a little pinch since she just requested it as I gather up my clothes, too.

Once we're dressed, I grab her into my arms, and we just stand in the basement in a hug for a few quiet moments.

"I should probably get to wrapping," I say.

She nods, and she perches back on the stool where we just fucked. Her cheeks are flushed, and she looks...happy. And freshly fucked. And gorgeous.

I wash my hands in the sink at the bar, and then I pull the first gift out of the bag. I packed Kelly's gifts in my carry-on, so I don't have to worry about her finding them down here. I do, however, have to figure out when to wrap them.

"She is going to love that," Kelly says as she eyes the stuffed girl pup from *Paw Patrol.* It's bigger than the one at Ellie's house, but not so big that I couldn't bring it here to Chicago.

The jumbo one is back at my place.

So I may have gone a little overboard since there was only a handful of people I needed to shop for.

I take out the other gifts I brought with me and feel confident that Mia is going to love all of them.

There's more upstairs in my suitcase. I wanted to bring something for Kelly's parents and grandparents, too. I wasn't quite sure what to get them, so I ended up going the sentimental route, which was never the route I took in the past.

And now I can't wait for them to open their gifts and see the reaction to what's inside.

But most of all, I can't wait to finally ask Kelly the question I came here to ask.

Chapter 29
Kelly Kaplan

Checking for Santa

Christmas Eve

I still can't quite believe he's here, even though the way he just rocked my world was sort of like pinching me to prove it's true.

I can honestly say I've never been railed in my grandparents' basement like that before.

"I feel bad," I say. "I didn't bring your gift here with me."

"You didn't need to get me anything. And I would never have expected you to bring it here since this was sort of a last-minute decision on my part."

"Well, thank God for last-minute decisions because I couldn't be happier to see you."

His eyes lift and meet mine. "I feel the exact same way." He leans down to press a kiss to my lips, and then he asks, "So...what are the sleeping arrangements?"

"The bed I sleep in is a queen, and Mia is in a travel crib, so there's room for you next to me."

"Is that okay?" he asks.

"Is what okay?"

"You know…sleeping in the same room, the same bed—in your grandparents' house." He averts his eyes back to the gift he's wrapping.

I lean in and whisper conspiratorially, "Considering Mia exists, I think they probably put two and two together."

"Still…don't they have rules?"

"If they do, nobody expressed them to me. I'm very much feeling like we should just apologize later if they're offended by the two of us sharing a bed, but I don't think they will be."

"That sounds like a good plan to me," he says. "If you're sure."

It's really sweet how he is thinking about what their potential rules might be and wanting to respect them, but I think after the conversations I've had with my family paired with the fact that I was going to take a redeye to get home to see him, they'll just be happy that we're together on Christmas.

I'm exhausted by the time we fall into bed beside each other. Between the emotions of being torn over whether or not to actually go home, finally making the decision only for my flight to be canceled, and then Austin showing up and draining every last bit of energy from my system, it's been quite the day.

Morning dawns, and I'm awake first. I sneak out of bed carefully so as not to wake either Austin or Mia, and I head downstairs. The house is quiet and dark, and I'm reminded of so many other Christmas mornings right here in this house.

I stand by the window and stare out as morning dawns. It's early here, but I don't get these cold, snowy mornings back home. The sun is hidden behind clouds, but the world is starting to lighten after the darkness of night. The landscape is covered in snow, and flakes still fall but more lazily now than they did last night.

"Merry Christmas," my mom says behind me, startling me. I jump and turn at the sound of her voice, and she comes in behind me to give me a little bear hug as my hand flies to my chest.

"Merry Christmas. You scared me."

She laughs. "What are you doing up so early?"

"Checking for Santa."

"I think he came last night," she says with a twinkle in her eye, and I know she means Austin, and I can't deny that it feels an awful lot like my Christmas wish came true.

My grandma comes down the stairs next, and it's three generations of women from the same bloodline in the room for a minute. Once Mia's awake, it'll be four, and there's something magical about having four wonderful females in the same room together.

"Is it true?" she asks as she walks over to the stovetop. She peels back the foil on something sitting there, and then she starts preheating the oven.

"Is what true?"

"There's a football player upstairs sleeping right now?" she asks.

I giggle. "Confirmed. But he's taken, so don't get any ideas."

She huffs in exasperation, but then she winks at me to let me know it's all in good fun. "I think your grandfather would have something to say about that anyway."

"What time is the baby getting up? Because I'm ready to start spoiling her," my mom asks.

I turn from the window and roll my eyes. "I think you probably spoiled her plenty this trip. I don't know how I'm ever going to get her home and return to normal eating with all the treats you keep giving her."

"Who's going to teach her the value of a good chocolate chip cookie if not for her grandmother?" my mom asks innocently.

"Oh, I don't know…maybe her aunt who owns the bakery where her mom works?" I tease.

"How is the bakery, by the way? How's work, and how's Ava?" my mom asks, and we sit down at the kitchen table as my grandma starts the pot of coffee.

"Good," I say. "Really good. Ava actually had me making wreaths for the decorations in the store. Some of the customers were interested in buying them, so I started making them on the side. We started getting more and more requests for them, and now I can hardly keep up with the demand."

"That's incredible," my dad says, appearing from out of nowhere. "Merry Christmas."

We all wish him a merry day back, and then I say, "Thank you. It's a fun hobby and one of my favorite things to do, but it's starting to take up a lot of time. I can't keep up with everything I need to do at the bakery and do this on the side…it's exhausting, to be honest."

"Have you gotten help for the baby?" my mom asks.

I nod. "We did a test run at a friend's house the other day. She has a nanny, and she watches a whole bunch of kids. Mia seemed to enjoy herself, and we got a good report back. Though you know how much I would love to have her grandparents close by to spend more time with her…" I trail off meaningfully since they're both in the room.

My mom was a kindergarten teacher for thirty-seven years before she retired. There's no one I would trust more to be with my little girl than her.

"I know, but with dad still working, we're not positioned to make a big move like that." It's been the same excuse ever since I asked them to move out, and I get it. It is a big change to go from Louisiana to Vegas, and even bigger since they're active in their community. I just wish they could be closer to us as Mia grows. I tried moving back to Louisiana when I was pregnant, but then being there means Mia doesn't get to be close to her dad. It's a tough balance.

Grandma puts the cinnamon buns in the oven, and just as it's starting to smell really good in here, Austin appears in the kitchen with Mia in his arms. She's smiling and jabbering "Dadada," and he's chuckling.

"Merry Christmas, everyone," he says, and my grandmother looks positively starstruck. It's the cutest dang thing I've ever seen.

We all say our good mornings, and my grandma serves up those cinnamon buns. My mom heated up a breakfast casserole, and we sit around my grandparents' table eating before presents— just like we always have. It's the magic of Christmas morning as I remember it from my childhood, but now my own child and the man I'm getting a second chance with get to experience it with me.

There's something pretty incredible about that.

Chapter 30
Austin Graham

I Love These Reindeer Pajama Pants

Christmas Morning

I help Kelly's dad drag two extra chairs into the family room so we can all gather by the tree, and Kelly's grandma tells us to take the love seat. We do, with Mia perched between us—for the moment, anyway. Kelly's grandpa turns on Christmas music, and her dad finds the Netflix fireplace channel, and it's all so…cozy. Idyllic. Perfect.

Similar to the vibe Kelly built at her own house.

It's what every parent wants for their kid. What every man wants for the woman he loves. It's all the things I associated with Christmas before my parents got divorced.

All I ever really wanted was the kind of warmth I feel here today. And maybe that's what I'll have in my future going forward—if everything goes as planned today, anyway.

I'm nervous as fuck, but I put on my game face. I have to.

Mia climbs off the couch—before the grandparents have even taken their seats yet—and she beelines right for a huge box wrapped in pink paper that has unicorns wearing Santa hats on it. At least she knows which box is for her. She starts clawing at the paper, and the four other adults aside from Kelly and myself turn their full attention to Mia as they beam at how talented she is at just under one year already opening her own gifts.

I scoot a little closer to Kelly, and I set my hand lightly on her thigh. I give it a little squeeze, and she looks over at me with a smile.

"Have I ever told you how much I love these reindeer pajama pants on you?" I ask, my voice low.

She giggles as she leans in toward me. "Have I ever told you how much I love *you*?"

I shake my head. "Not today."

She leans in closer still, lowering her voice to be sure only I hear her. "I thought I showed you that pretty well last night."

I put up my hand for a high-five, and she slaps my palm with hers as we both laugh.

Her mom glances over at us, a little smile playing at her lips, and I know she feels it, too—the warmth in here. The love in here. The absolute perfection of this morning that's only going to get better.

Mia gets the box open and seems pretty damn excited about the musical instrument playset that someone was gracious enough to put batteries in before wrapping.

We listen to the loud, grating sounds of guitar and drums and organ the way only an almost one-year-old can play them.

Kelly leans over to me again. "Damn. I think it might be too big to fit into any of our suitcases, so I guess we'll have to leave it here."

I laugh, and Kelly's mom passes out presents for each of us to open—including me.

I give her a surprised look. "You didn't have to do that," I say.

"I was sending it home with Kelly anyway." She smiles and shrugs, and the way she can so easily make me feel like I'm a part of this family even though Kelly and I just got back together is really special.

I tear it open and find a custom cutting board with *GRAHAM 41* engraved on it. I feel oddly emotional over something that's just a piece of wood, and yet…it means so much more than that.

It means someone thought of me. It means someone considered the things I like, the things that are important to me, and then they placed an order for something special.

A thick lump forms in my throat as I stare down at the board. Nobody has ever given me a gift like this before, and I'm not quite sure how to respond. I'm used to clothes I'll never wear or video games or generic items I could just buy for myself.

This has meaning behind it.

"Kel said you like to cook," her mom says. "We hope you like it."

"I love it," I say, my voice a whisper as her mom smiles warmly at me.

Kelly reaches over and sets her hand on my thigh this time, and it seems to mark the moment when I feel true acceptance for maybe the first time in my life. I feel like a part of the family, and it's a powerful, wonderful feeling.

We laugh as we watch Mia, who definitely has the most gifts under the tree, tear into all of them, and we smile as we watch each other open our gifts.

Kelly's mom hands her a huge box, and Kelly laughs as she says, "I have no idea how we're going to get all this home."

She tears open the paper to find a box covered in packing tape. She finds the scissors and slits open the tape only to find another wrapped box inside.

And another, and another.

Her parents are looking at her with twinkling eyes when she finally gets down to the final box and pulls out a piece of paper.

She gasps and holds a hand over her mouth for a second. "For real?" she asks.

Both her parents are grinning and nodding when she leaps to her feet to hug them both, and I grab the piece of paper she left behind in the box.

Surprise! We're moving to Vegas!

My chest warms at the thought that we'll have actual *family* nearby. What a gift.

"This is the best Christmas *ever!*" Kelly says, and she doesn't even know the half of it yet.

When we get down to the final three gifts under the tree, I get up to pass them out. They're all the same, and I give one to Kelly's grandma, one to Kelly's mom, and one to Kelly.

"You can open them at the same time," I say, and Kelly glances at the other women in the room before she tears into hers.

Her eyes shine brightly with tears when she looks up at me after seeing the gift inside—a canvas print of our very first family photo together, the one where we're all wearing our matching gingerbread man sweaters and standing by the Christmas tree on a day that felt like the start of a family tradition for us.

"This is so thoughtful, Austin," Kelly's mom says as she stares down at the photo and wipes away the tears splashing onto her cheeks.

That lump is back in my throat again, and I need to get a handle on my emotions or I'll never get through the final gift.

"Merry Christmas, everyone," Kelly's dad says. "Thank you all for the thoughtful gifts. Now let's make some hot cocoa with peppermint schnapps!"

The adults all get up to get a start on what sounds like their next tradition, but I speak up. "Wait!"

Everyone freezes where they are.

"There's one more," I say.

Kelly's mom inspects the space under the tree, but it's empty. Everyone looks at me in confusion, and I draw in a deep breath.

"I, uh…" I begin, and I think I black out for a second as I try to remember what the fuck I wanted to say. "Thank you all for allowing me to crash your Christmas. This is the nicest, warmest, most wonderful Christmas morning I think I've ever had in my life."

Kelly stands and slings her arm around my waist, and I lean down to press a kiss to the top of her head as my heart races.

"I'd like to be a part of all of your Christmas mornings," I say, looking down at her. Her brown eyes lift to mine, and warmth radiates from her as I turn in and take her into my arms in front of the people who mean the most to her in the whole world. "In some ways, this feels too soon. In other ways, it's been coming since the night I met you at the Gridiron almost two years ago. I love you, Kelly Kaplan. I love our daughter, and I love the life we're building together. I love your family. I struck out with my own family, but sometimes we're lucky enough to get to pick the people who become our family. And this is the one I pick. It's the one I want to be in forever."

I get down on one knee and pull the ring out of my pocket where it has nestled since I woke up this morning.

My hands are trembling as I hold the ring out in front of me. "Will you marry me?"

Her hands fly to her mouth in shock as she gasps, and then she shakes them out. "Oh my God! Yes!" She holds her left hand out, and I slide the ring onto her finger. She admires it for only a quick second as I rise to a stand, and she leaps against me, her mouth crashing to mine as we celebrate this moment.

It's one more core memory created because of her, and as we kiss to the sound of clapping and whooping in the room, I get this sense of déjà vu for something that hasn't even happened yet as I picture the two of us sealing our vows with a kiss at our wedding as our guests clap and whoop all around us.

It's just the beginning of the future I never knew I could have, and I definitely don't deserve, but I plan to spend the rest of my days grateful for all of it anyway.

Chapter 31
Kelly Kaplan

The Best Christmas Ever

Christmas Day

I can't stop staring at the pear-shaped sparkler on my finger.

It's the best Christmas of my life, that's for sure. I came here with a boyfriend, and I'm leaving with a fiancé.

I'm getting *married*. I'm going to be a *wife*.

It's incredible. It's crazy. It's unexpected, and somehow it's everything I never knew I wanted. I can't wait to spend the rest of my life with the man who—let's be honest—I've been in love with for the better part of a year and a half.

I text Ava to wish her a Merry Christmas, and I can't help but add in a little something extra.

Me: *Merry Christmas, bestie! I can't wait to get home and tell you what Austin gave me.*

Ava: *Merry Christmas! If it's his dick, you know I'm here for all the details.*

I giggle as I read her message. She's a far cry from the virgin she was the night she met Grayson Nash, and I think he's left a bit of an influence on her. Among other things, I'm sure.

Me: *Only if you count getting railed in my grandparents' basement while everyone else was sleeping.*

Ava: *I'll be sure to thank Lincoln later when I see him for giving the boys the day off. He showed up in Chicago?*

Me: *He did, and that's a whole other story.*

Ava: *I can't wait to hear it.*

Me: *I'll see you next week!*

I have no idea how I'm going to keep this a secret from my best friend until I'm back home, but I know I need to wait to see the look on her face when I tell her the news.

Austin chuckles, and I glance over at him.

"What?"

"That's what you two text each other?" he asks.

Everyone else is distracted by *A Miracle on 34th Street* as it plays on the television at a volume way too high for anyone under the age of thirty, and Mia is upstairs napping after a wild morning.

My cheeks grow hot as I realize he read her message about his dick. I lift a shoulder as I pretend like I'm not totally embarrassed. "We share everything. Except partners."

"Good, because you're the one I want to be with."

"You hit on her first," I say, and I'm not sure *why* I say it. It just sort of falls out of my mouth.

He leans his forehead to my temple. "Only because I didn't think I stood a chance in hell with you."

Okay, fine. The line works.

I wish this could last a little longer, but he has to catch a flight back to Vegas tonight so he can get up and go to practice tomorrow.

That's when I realize…I want to go with him.

He has an entire offseason where we can travel together. We could spend a month in Louisiana with my parents if we wanted to, or we could come here to Chicago to spend time with my grandparents. I don't want to miss his game this Sunday, and I don't want to miss *him*.

I don't want to say goodbye.

"Are you sure you can't come with me?" he asks a little while later once Mia is up and he's packing his bag. He glances up at me and twists his lips a little, and I finally voice the words I've been thinking all day.

"Okay." I shrug.

"Okay what?" His brows crash together in confusion.

"Okay, I'll come with you."

He looks surprised for a second, and then he narrows his eyes at me. "Are you just fucking with me?"

I shake my head as I start to throw my stuff in a suitcase along with Mia's. "Nope. I hope you weren't just being nice because Mia and I are coming home with you."

He stares at me for a beat, and then he strides over and takes me in his arms. "Just when I thought this Christmas couldn't get any better…" He trails off, and his lips fall to mine, and *damn*, this really is the best Christmas ever. "Oh, I almost forgot with the excitement of the engagement, but I actually got you something else."

My brows dip. "What is it?"

He pulls an envelope out of his suitcase and hands it over to me. "This."

Our eyes connect for a beat, and he looks like he's up to some mischief. I slide my finger along the back of the envelope to open it, and I pull out a couple of papers.

I read the top of the first one. *State of Nevada Business License.*

My eyes move to the next line. *Kaplan's Crafts.*

The next page is a document for an LLC in the name of Kaplan's Crafts, and the final page is a bank account in my name with fifty thousand dollars in it.

"Kaplan's Crafts?" I ask, confusion evident on my face as I glance up at him.

"Your new wreath business. You know…if you want it." He looks a little unsure.

"If I want it?" I repeat, still not quite sure what he's talking about.

"You once told me you wished you could make wreaths all day, but you had a job to do at the bakery. Well, what if making wreaths *was* your job?"

Tears pinch behind my eyes. "You created a business for me?" He nods.

"I can't accept this," I say, handing the bank statement back to him. "This is way too much, Austin. It's…what, like a couple hundred bucks for supplies? What am I going to do with all that money?"

He hands the paper back to me. "It's an investment for our future, Kel. You'll have what you need to get started, and if you want to open a store down the road, the money will be there to help. And this gives you the cushion not to feel like you have to keep working at the bakery if you don't want to."

I nod a little as I snag my bottom lip between my teeth. The bakery has come to feel like a second home to me, and I don't really want to give up working with my best friend.

But I also love the idea of finally, *finally* finding something of my own. Something that will give me my own purpose aside from the very important job of *mom*. Something I can grow and nurture and enjoy as Mia grows, too.

"Thank you," I whisper, and I brush a tear away. "This is really thoughtful, Austin."

"I just want you to be happy, and when you're making your wreaths, you're happy."

I rush into his arms, and he lets out a little *oof* of surprise. "You make me happy." I tilt my head and rise to my tiptoes to press my lips to his.

"I'll do whatever I can to make sure you feel that way every single day."

"You're off to a good start." I kiss him once more, and then I let out a contented sigh before I turn my attention back to packing.

It's a lot to think about, but today has been filled with all the things that I want for my future.

He set an awfully high bar this Christmas, and it's not something I'll ever forget.

Chapter 32
Kelly Kaplan

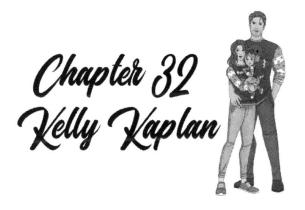

Talk Like a Pirate Day

The Day After Christmas

I draw in a deep breath as I pull open the door to the bakery.

"Oh my God, Kelly! What are you doing here?" Ava asks from just behind the counter when she sees me walk in.

It's the bakery's downtime—not *off* time since that doesn't exist, but less crowded than the rush times—and she rounds the counter to give me a hug.

"I came home with Austin," I say with a grin. I pull out of our hug and flash my hand at her, and she grabs it and screams.

"Oh my God!" she squeals. "He proposed?"

"He did!" I squeal back.

"And you said yes?"

"I did!"

"Ahh! Congratulations!" She jumps up and down with her hands on my forearms, and I jump up and down with her.

We come to a stop, and we hug again.

"Thank you! And you know I need you to be my matron of honor, but we haven't set a date or even talked about it yet. It's all just so surreal still."

He walks in behind me carrying both Mia and the gift bag with a present for Ava.

"I'm so happy for you two!" Ava says, hugging him next and pressing a kiss to Mia's cheek as she steals her from Austin's arms. She makes silly faces at Mia, who giggles like she always does when her Auntie Ava is holding her.

"Thanks," he says to Ava. He turns to me with a twinkle in his eye. "You made quick work of that."

I lift a shoulder with a smile as I take the present from him. I hand the bag over to Ava. "This is for you."

"Oof, it's heavy," she says, and she hands Mia back to Austin as she carries it over to the counter. She digs through the tissue paper I stuck inside, and she pulls out a bottle of vodka and a bag of Doritos—Cool Ranch, our favorite.

She laughs, her eyes sparkling, and she leans in for a hug. "You're so sweet, Kel. Stay right here. I got you something, too."

She disappears into the back and returns with a gift bag a moment later.

I tear out the tissue paper, too, and I find a bottle of vodka and a bag of Cool Ranch Doritos inside.

"You really are two of a kind, aren't you?" Austin says, and the two of us just laugh. We know what we like, and there's nothing wrong with that.

"I got Mia a few things, too. They're in my office if you want to come on back," Ava tells us, and we follow her back to her office, where we find a huge box. And by huge, I mean at least four feet by four feet, and that's not the only gift in here.

"What did you do?" I ask.

She giggles and shrugs. "Sorry. I couldn't help but spoil my girl."

I tear off the wrapping paper and find a backyard wooden playhouse inside, and the next box has all sorts of goodies to decorate the house, like stuffed animals, pillows, and play mats.

"You didn't have to do all this, but she's going to love it once Austin puts it together," I tease, and Austin gives me a look in jest.

"It'll be perfect in the room I'm planning to turn into a playroom for her," he says, elbowing me a little, and I laugh.

"Cookie," Mia says, and all three of us turn toward her.

"Did you just say *cookie*?" I ask.

"Cookie!" Mia says again.

"Oh my gosh, she said *cookie*!" I squeal, and Austin picks her up and twirls her around.

"I think she deserves a cookie since she asked for one," he says, and he carries her out toward the counter so she can pick one out.

"So the holidays are over now. Are you ready to move in with him?" Ava asks, nodding toward his retreating figure.

"I'm ready. And I need to talk to you about something else."

"Uh oh. This looks serious." She perches on the edge of her desk. "What's going on?"

"Um…I'm not sure how to say this." I stand in place and fidget with my ring, twisting it around for a few beats before I glance up and find her watching me carefully.

"Are you leaving me?" she asks. "Because I can take it if you are. I knew this wouldn't last forever."

"No! No. Except…" I trail off. "Yes. Kind of. Not permanently. I don't know."

"Spit it out, Kaplan," she demands.

I clear my throat. "I need to cut back hours. Significantly. I'm going to start a wreath business, but I don't want to give up what we have here, so I can still help out with scheduling and things. Whatever the most important tasks are that you need me to handle, I'm here. But I also understand if you need to hire someone else full-time."

Her jaw drops a little as I babble. "Wait a minute, wait a minute. You're starting a wreath business?"

"Kaplan's Crafts. Actually, Austin gifted me the business license and some other stuff for Christmas."

"Holy smokes, Kel. An engagement ring and a business? How's he ever going to top this one?"

I lift a shoulder and make a face. "I'm not sure. A monthlong trip to Hawaii, maybe?"

She laughs, and she jumps down from her desk and gives me another hug. "I'm so happy for you, and honestly, you can work as much or as little as you want. I love, love, *love* working with you, but I'm excited to see what you can do with your wreaths. I always knew you were destined for greater things than sitting in an office."

I set my hands on her upper arms. "But you gave me the job that allowed me to work the entire first year of my daughter's life with her right by my side, and I will never be able to thank you enough for that."

"Oh! Wait! What if I gave you a rack or two in the café to sell stuff from while you get things up and running?" she suggests.

"I couldn't ask you to do that," I say, shaking my head.

"Why not? You're already selling stuff out of my bakery anyway. May as well give you some prime real estate. And make some Vegas Aces wreaths. Dude, people would go *nuts* for those." She raises her brows. "My mom had a different wreath on our front door every holiday when I was growing up. They don't have to be limited to just Christmas, you know. Valentine's Day, Memorial Day…hell, Flag Day, *ooh,* Talk Like a Pirate Day—they all need wreaths."

"Talk Like a Pirate Day?" I repeat, narrowing my eyes at her.

"What? It's totally a thing. Ask Grayson. And ask him what he did to me on that day last year." She wiggles her eyebrows suggestively, and I don't doubt he dressed up like a pirate and saved the damsel in distress with his…peg leg.

Austin walks back into the office, and he's holding Mia, who's eating a cookie with green and red frosting on it. He clearly took a bite since he has a little bit of green frosting on the side of his mouth, and he also has some red garland around his neck that Mia is playing with as she eats her cookie.

I stare at these two loves of my life as this wave of pure happiness washes over me. Two months ago, back when Austin was being a scrooge since he felt like he was second best in every aspect of his life, I never would've seen us here. Our journey has been filled with bad timing and tough choices, but my second down Scrooge and I are finally on the same page, and I can't wait to build our future together.

Epilogue
Austin Graham

Did Cupid Throw Up in Here

Two Weeks Later

I stare at the mess on the kitchen table, and I can't help but laugh. "Did Cupid throw up in here?"

Kelly glances up at me as she loops some red meshy shit back and forth on a wire frame. "Sorry. I promise I'll clean this up before we get Mia."

I walk over to her and shake my head. "I'm just teasing you. What can I do?"

She sighs, and she finishes pulling the meshy shit through the frame. "I'm not sure. I have three more of these Valentine's wreaths to make, and I wanted to do little mini wreaths with unicorns and rainbows for Mia's birthday party next weekend with my business card attached, but I'm running out of time."

"I can't believe she's turning one a week from tomorrow," I say. "And I'll do whatever I can to help you get it all done. Are you going into the bakery this week?"

She nods and picks up another frame and more of the red netting. "Just for a couple hours on Friday, and I'd like to have

201

these Valentine's ones ready when I go in. Oh, that reminds me, Lakeside called with the dates they have available."

"And?" I ask. Lakeside is her dream wedding venue, and we agreed that whatever date they have open is the date we're doing it.

"And they had a cancellation for April fourth."

It should make me shudder. That's just under three months away.

But there's nothing scary about marrying this woman. In fact, I can't wait.

"Do they have anything sooner?" I ask playfully, and she laughs as I lean down to kiss her.

"I think that's the soonest, babe. I booked it, and I texted Desi, who is pulling all the strings for us." Over the last couple of weeks, I guess Kelly and Desiree, the woman Asher is marrying, have gotten close, and Kelly apparently already tapped Desi to plan our wedding since she's an event planner.

"Four-four. It has a nice ring to it."

"And you'll put a ring on it," she jokes. "Tell me about your day."

I sit in the chair next to her and start to organize the pink foam hearts by size and color. "My day started with a light workout, and then I went in for some treatment. We had some meetings, did a little film study, and did a walk-through. And now I'm here."

"Treatment for what?"

"My back. You know how it's been sore since the game after Christmas, so I went in for a massage."

She looks up at me with a raised brow and pursed lips, and I chuckle.

"There's literally nothing sexual about getting a massage in the locker room, least of all when it's Hector giving the treatment."

"That's better."

I lean over and press a kiss to her cheek. "Even if it was Alison, it still wouldn't be sexual, babe. You're the only one who gets to give me the happy ending."

"You're damn right about that. Speaking of which…" She sets down the frame she's working on. "We need to pick up Mia in less than an hour, so if you want to—"

I don't let her finish that sentence because of fucking course I want to.

I lift to a stand and pull her out of her chair and into my arms.

She laughs. "I was going to say if you want to figure out a plan for dinner, but this works, too," she says as I carry her across the house and up the stairs.

I take her into our bedroom and throw her onto the bed, and she's grinning as I move to hover over her. I run my lips along her neck. "God, you taste good," I say as I thrust my hips to hers, and she's not laughing anymore as she moans, stretching her neck back as she closes her eyes and folds to the pleasure.

My lips move to hers, and it's as we kiss that I can see our future together. I see Christmases with matching sweaters and more kids and so much laughter. I see the warmth Kelly radiates as I bask in it and actually *enjoy* the holiday as an adult when so many of those moments were stripped from my past.

I see everything I didn't know was within my reach for my own future as I saw everyone around me getting those things.

"Want me to go on top since your back's hurting?" she asks, and it's like the goddamn magic question to ask a man as he's gearing up for sex.

"Fuck yeah, I do," I say, and I climb off her, pull her heart pajama pants down her legs, and pull my own jeans off as she shimmies out of her sweatshirt.

Once we're both naked, I lay on the bed, and she climbs over me.

I run my hands along her torso and up to those perfect tits of hers, where I allow my hands to explore and tease as she fists my cock and lines her body up with mine. She slides down onto me, and her pussy is so hot, so wet, so tight. It's utter perfection as she starts to move, and her on top is always a treat since it tickles all of my senses. I love to watch her as her face contorts with pleasure and her tits bounce up and down. I love to peek down between us where our bodies are connected as I see my shaft disappearing into her sweet cunt. I love to listen to her sounds, to taste her skin, to touch her tits, to smell the cinnamon scent of her perfume that lingers long after the Christmas season is over.

I love everything about her, and as my body tightens up in advance of an explosive release inside her, I can't help but feel an overwhelming sense of gratitude that she's the person I get to do this with for the rest of my life.

I come first to someone now, and it means everything to me. So much, in fact, that I *literally* come first, and it propels her into her own release. She leans down to claw at my chest for balance as she bounces over my cock, moaning my name as she comes.

As it turns out, our second chance at love was the best gift this Christmas, and I will work every day for the rest of my life to make sure she knows she and the life we're building together come first to me too.

Want more Kelly and Austin? Scan this QR code to download a bonus epilogue!

Scan this code to join
Team LS: Lisa Suzanne's Reader Group!

Acknowledgments

Thank you first as always to my husband! Thanks for inventing hours for me to write, for supporting me, and for being the best dad to our sweet babies. I love having you as part of my team, and I love the family we've created together.

Thank you Valentine PR for your incredible work on the launch of this series and this book.

Thank you to Valentine Grinstead, Diane Holtry, Christine Yates, Billie DeSchalit, and Serena Cracchiolo for beta and proofreading. I value your insight and comments so much.

Thank you to Renee McCleary for all you do.

Thank you to my ARC Team for loving this sports world that is so real to us. Thank you to the members of the Vegas Aces Spoiler Room and Team LS, and all the influencers and bloggers for reading, reviewing, posting, and sharing.

And finally, thank YOU for reading. I can't wait to bring more football and more Nash family! I'm so excited for what's coming next!

Cheers until next season!

xoxo,

Lisa Suzanne

About the Author

Lisa Suzanne is an Amazon Top Ten Bestselling author of swoon-worthy superstar heroes, emotional roller coasters, and all the angst. She resides in Arizona with her husband and two kids. When she's not chasing her kids, she can be found working on her latest romance book or watching reruns of *Friends*.

Also by Lisa Suzanne

DATING THE DEFENSIVE BACK
(The Nash Brothers #1)

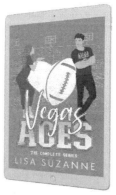

VEGAS ACES: THE COMPLETE SERIES

FIND MORE AT AUTHORLISASUZANNE.COM/BOOKS